Cameron froze. **and pulled away** ~~...ing.~~

Cameron lost her grip and fell through the air. She pushed off, hoping she could land on solid ground. The thought was great in theory—she didn't relish pain—but it wasn't very practical, since construction debris lay scattered across the ground at her feet. Her grandfather would have cringed over the negligence of the work site's safety conditions. It hadn't seemed to matter…until now.…

She closed her eyes, waiting for impact. Instead, a strong set of arms caught her. The momentum knocked her close against a strong, solid chest.

"It's okay. I've got you," Seth whispered. His mouth was inches from her ear and his spearmint-scented breath moved across her cheek.

It figured. After all his teasing about not falling from the ladder, she'd not only fallen, but he'd had to run to her rescue! She'd never live this down.

PAIGE WINSHIP DOOLY

is the author of over a dozen books and novellas. She enjoys living in the coastal Deep South with her family, after having grown up in the sometimes extremely cold Midwest. She is happily married to her high school sweetheart and loves their life of adventure in a full house with six homeschooled children and two dogs.

Books by Paige Winship Dooly

HEARTSONG PRESENTS

Special Delivery

Paige Winship Dooly

Heartsong Presents

To my husband Troy. Thanks so much for your constant support and encouragement in both writing and life. I love you!

A note from the Author:

I love to hear from my readers! You may correspond with me by writing:

Paige Winship Dooly
Author Relations
P.O. Box 9048
Buffalo, NY 14240-9048

ISBN-13: 978-0-373-48637-3

SPECIAL DELIVERY

This edition issued by special arrangement with Barbour Publishing, Inc., 1810 Barbour Drive, Uhrichsville, Ohio, U.S.A.

Chapter 1

"I don't know, Cam. There are so many other things you could do to help that don't involve working with those high windows. Seems like we're asking for trouble." Seth put his hands on his hips and surveyed the ladder in question. "Yep, this looks like a job for the big boys." His voice held a hint of amusement as he teased her—and he underscored his comment with a wink—but Cam knew that ultimately, he meant what he said.

It annoyed her. She understood that Seth was used to taking charge and watching out for his elderly aunt, but Cameron was neither elderly nor was she his charge. He knew good and well that Cameron was every bit as capable as a man when it came to climbing up the ladder and doing the job set before her, but he was the knight-in-shining-armor type who apparently felt the need to protect the females around him.

Cam folded her arms across her chest and dug in.

"Seth. I'm painting the trim on an upper window. It's not like we want the kids up there doing that. I hardly think my painting from a ladder should be an issue."

"I didn't call it an issue. I just said there are other—safer—avenues for you to pursue if you're determined to help."

"Why wouldn't I help?" Cameron asked, perplexed. "Didn't we all come here as a youth group to fix up the houses and yards?"

Cameron glanced around for an ally. Her friend Josie shrugged and with an upturned hand waved her away. She wasn't getting in the middle of things.

Cameron turned back to Seth with raised eyebrows and waited for his answer.

"Yes, Cameron. We did come to fix up houses and yards." He sounded like he was talking to one of the teens—one of the very *young* teens. "There's way more yard than house. You have plenty of options to choose from. Find somewhere else—somewhere safer—to work." Seth placed both hands on his hips and glared at the window, as if it were responsible for placing the irritating woman in front of him. "Find something safe to do, somewhere else. How about you go pull some weeds over there with Josie? She looks like she's having fun."

They both looked over at Josie.

"Time of my life." Josie rolled her eyes. "And stop trying to drag me into your squabbles."

"We aren't squabbling." Seth snorted. "We're discussing."

Cameron put her hands on her hips. "Actually—we are squabbling."

"No. We aren't."

They stood facing each other, both with hands on hips now, mirroring each other's actions.

"Then why are you taking issue with my helping out? I'm one of the youth leaders. I volunteered to work, and I intend to work."

"Look, why don't you sit over there with Mandy and visit with the owner?" Seth stepped closer to Cameron. He pointed at the two women but didn't give her a chance to respond. "Mandy looks perfectly happy entertaining our elderly host."

"Right, so that job position is covered." Cameron momentarily lost focus as she glanced at his lips and noticed that they were far too close to her own. She and Seth were almost nose to nose. If she tipped the slightest bit forward, she'd feel his lips touch hers. Were they really as soft as they looked? One thing was for sure, he was every bit as good-looking when yelling at her from two inches away as he was when he was yelling at her from four feet away.

Josie snickered, breaking the moment. Busted! Drats! Her friend had caught her staring at Seth and apparently read her thoughts. Were her emotions that obvious? Could Seth read them, too? She pushed aside the distracting questions and squared her shoulders.

Yelling was most definitely the safer way of expressing her feelings at the moment. Cameron tried to remember what they'd been yelling about. Oh yeah, he'd suggested she sit primly with the pregnant girl and the elderly lady while everyone else did the hard stuff. "Do I really need to point out that Mandy is almost eight months pregnant? She has no choice in the matter. She can't exactly climb ladders to paint or nail shingles in her condition."

"My point exactly." Seth backed off and paced the

area, apparently ready to move on to other projects. "If you join her, we'll be sure she remains safe and out of the way."

"She's already safe and out of the way. Or do you think *I'm* the one in the way?"

"I didn't say you were in the way." Exasperation laced his words. "I love having you here."

Her heart skipped a beat. "You do?" The traitorous words came out on a breathless note.

"Hey Seth," Matt called from the roof, interrupting the moment, "why don't you accept defeat and give the girl a shot?"

Catcalls came from various places around the house. One voice yelled over the others. "Yeah Seth, give the girl a shot."

Cameron cringed. "I think they misunderstood Matt's wording."

"Oh no they didn't." Seth grinned at her. "They know exactly what he meant, and they know exactly what they're doing."

"Then why did they—oh." She blushed. "They're trying to embarrass us."

"And they're apparently succeeding when it comes to you."

"I'm not embarrassed."

"Then why are you blushing?"

Cameron's hand involuntarily went to her face. "I've been out in the sun for hours, Seth. Don't read anything into it...."

"And you didn't use sunscreen? I'd think a nurse would know better. Not healthy, Cam."

"I *used* sunscreen! I'm flushed from the heat. It's hot out here. I just—oh, never mind."

Josie's soft laugh carried from the flower bed where

she worked a few feet away. She squatted in front of the flowers, an amused expression on her face.

"Don't you have weeds to pull or something, Josie?"

Josie turned away. "Pulling them now." She held up a handful of plants to prove her point.

Seth crossed his arms. His feet were spread shoulder width apart. With the sun behind him, putting him in silhouette, he looked like a warrior ready to do battle. "*If* I let you climb up the ladder, will you promise not to fall off?"

"If you *let* me?" Cameron scowled up at him. "Last I checked I was an adult—fully capable of making my own decisions."

"Ohh, she got you there, boss."

Seth stared down the senior who'd made the comment and motioned with his thumb for him to move on. The boy smirked and continued toward the back of the house with the armload of firewood he'd just chopped.

"So, as I was saying… Do you think you can promise—"

"It's kind of hard to promise when falling is something you don't exactly plan for." With a sigh Cameron elbowed past him and skittered up the ladder before he could repeat the obnoxious question. She studied her work area. "I need to fix the nails in the trim before I can paint. They're sticking out." She turned around and held her hand out for the hammer.

Seth rolled his eyes and slapped it into her hand. "That's what I like to see, an enthusiastic worker."

"I've been trying to work for a quarter of an hour." Cameron flipped the hammer into the air and caught it, her eyes never leaving Seth's face.

"I'm impressed." Seth raised his eyebrows. "You

obviously know your way around both a hammer *and* a ladder."

"Thanks for noticing. My grandfather was a master carpenter. Apparently he found me a bit difficult to handle once I hit my teen years. As a result, I spent many an hour working by his side while on restriction."

"Why does that not surprise me?" Seth laughed and held tight to the ladder.

She slipped the hammer into a loop on her cargo pants and climbed another rung.

The ladder shifted.

"Whoa there!" He tightened his grip and held the ladder steady as she continued her ascent, climbing like the professional she was. "You sure you can stay on this thing?"

She glanced down at him and acted as if the movement hadn't fazed her. "I think a better question would be, can you promise not to *let* me fall off the ladder?"

"Sorry. Can't do that. Once I get you stable, I need to go check on the kids out back. Caleb had to run to the store, and Matt is on the roof. I need to see how they're doing."

"No problem. I'll be fine."

The ladder shifted again.

"Or not!" Cameron clutched the rails. "Seth? Are you doing that on purpose?"

"Just making sure she's solid. I don't think she's going anywhere." Seth hesitated. "Do you want me to find someone to hold it for you? I'm sure Josie can help for a few minutes. Right, Josie?"

"No. Don't bother her. I'll be fine." The last thing she needed was Josie having nothing but time to grill Cameron about her earlier conversation with Seth. "We all have jobs to do, and Josie needs to get hers finished, too. Go do what you have to do. I know it doesn't pay to leave the munchkins unattended."

"I agree." Reluctantly, he backed away and wove his way around the construction debris, heading for the back of the house.

Cam couldn't resist taking a moment to enjoy the view. Seth was certainly easy on the eyes. His dark brown hair dusted against his collar, the golden highlights attesting to hours in the sun. His blue work shirt pulled tight across his wide shoulders, accentuating the muscles he'd earned through hard work. His long powerful legs ate up the distance as he walked around the side of the house with an easy stride.

With a smile, Cameron moved one step higher on the ladder. Time to get back to work…after one more quick peek. Cameron leaned to the right for a final glimpse before Seth rounded the back corner of the house. The ladder slid along with her. With a yelp, she leaned to the left to right herself. She overcorrected and grabbed the window frame to stop the momentum.

"Like what you see up there, hon? Must be quite a view." Josie stood watching her with a hand shading her eyes.

Cameron startled at Josie's question, which threw the ladder back off-balance. She shrieked as the ladder slid farther to the left. She counteracted the movement with her body, but the momentum only slowed. The ladder balanced precariously, and it was a toss-up which way it would go. "Oh, this so isn't good."

"Don't move…. I'll get Seth."

"No!" Cameron shrieked again. "Don't you dare. Not after that hard time he gave me about my being up here. I mean, you don't need to bother him. You and I can handle this. We'll be fine. Just secure the ladder for a minute, and I'll climb down and reposition it."

Josie grabbed the ladder, but her petite figure was no match for gravity. "I can't hold you, Cam. I don't want to let you fall."

Cameron tried to ease down a rung, but the movement made the ladder slide farther.

"Cam, stop moving! I can't hold you. Seth!" Josie's screech was loud enough to be heard throughout the lower Ozark Mountains.

Cameron froze. The ladder twisted and pulled away from the building. Cameron lost her grip and fell through the air. She pushed off, hoping she could land on solid ground. The thought was great in theory—she didn't relish pain—but it wasn't very practical, since construction debris lay scattered across the ground at her feet. Her grandfather would have cringed over the negligence of the work site's safety conditions. It hadn't seemed to matter...until now.

The force of the ladder had her falling at a backward angle, and she knew she'd never find her footing from this position. She set her jaw, bracing herself for the pain of landing on a brick or a piece of wood with a nail sticking through it.

She closed her eyes, waiting for impact. Instead, a strong set of arms caught her. The momentum knocked her close against a strong, solid chest.

"It's okay. I've got you." Seth whispered. His mouth was inches from her ear and his spearmint-scented breath moved across her cheek.

It figured. After all his teasing about not falling from the ladder, she'd not only fallen, but he'd had to run to her rescue! She'd never live this down.

Unfortunately, his arms were full with her, and

he couldn't prevent the momentum of the ladder that slammed against her shoulder on its way past.

"Ohhh, that hurt," Cameron muttered through clenched teeth.

The ladder rotated and clipped Seth's head.

"Ah… So did that." Seth groaned.

"I'll get the first aid kit." Josie hurried away to collect it.

A circle of spectators formed around them.

"That was *so* romantic!" Sailor gushed from behind them. "Did you see the whole thing, Mandy? Seth heard Cam's scream and flew into action. I've never seen anyone move so fast. And look at how gently he's holding her. Precious!"

"I know!" Mandy crooned back, her green eyes soft as she held her hand against her mouth. Her brown ponytail whipped through the air as she spun her head around to look in Sailor's direction. "And the way he caught her. It was amazing. He's cradling her in his arms. So sweet!"

"We're standing right here," Seth growled.

"So we see." Mandy's voice was far too smug. "Standing there all cuddly-like—clutching Cam against your big strong chest. Nice."

Cameron realized Mandy was right. Seth still held her against him, like she'd fall apart if he set her down. She turned to face him. "I'm fine, Seth. I can stand on my own. You can put me down."

Big mistake, this turning thing. It once again put them face-to-face. Only this time, Seth was holding her in his arms. His blue-green eyes were far too close to hers. Cam could see little specks of dark blue in their depths. His pupils dilated, widening as their eyes made contact. Cameron lost her breath. Again she wondered

what it would be like to kiss him—wondered if he'd
dare kiss her. She wished he would.

Her tunnel vision cleared, and she took in the group
of spectators gathered around them. Kissing would *not*
be a good thing. What was she thinking? Though it had
been a year since her husband had walked out on her,
she wasn't sure she was ready to face a new relationship. Maybe the ladder had grazed her head, too. Regardless of her muddled thoughts, Seth didn't seem to
be in any hurry to force her from his arms.

Matt's voice intruded and shattered the moment as
he pushed his way through the crowd. "Show's over,
kids. Get back to your positions." He turned to Seth
and Cameron. "You two okay? I saw the tail end of the
show from the roof after Cameron screamed."

"It wasn't a show, and I didn't scream!"

Josie appeared with the first aid kit. "She's right. It
was more of a shriek."

"But it had him running." Mandy sighed. "Her very
own knight in shining armor. Way to go, Cam."

"Mandy. Please. As your nurse-midwife, I'm asking you to go sit down. Too much excitement at this
point isn't healthy for you." Cameron pointed to Mandy's chair.

"I'm fine." Mandy grinned. "Healthy as a horse. You
said so yourself at my appointment this morning."

The elderly woman who owned the house finally
made her way to their side. "Let me look at your shoulder, dear. That ladder clipped you pretty good."

Did anyone miss Cameron's fall?

Seth finally set her on her feet. She wobbled, either
because of the fall or because of Seth's strong arm still
wrapped around her waist.

"Thank you, but I'll be fine." Cam waved the woman

away. "I'll probably have a bruise, but it's nothing compared to what Seth's head must feel like. Let me look
at it, Seth."

"I'm fine, too." Seth tried to push her away.

"You're not fine. You're bleeding. You might have a
concussion. Let me check it out." She pushed his hair
out of the way. Her fingers tingled where they touched
his scalp.

Two dozen teens stood in a circle around them,
watching with undisguised interest.

"Back to work, now!" Cameron ordered, her hospital persona kicking in.

The kids scampered back to their jobs. Matt gave
her two thumbs up.

"I'm too short to see your cut. You need to sit down."

Surprisingly, Seth allowed her to lead him to a
nearby bench without a fight. The homeowner had
brought out a bowl of cool water. Cameron bathed the
wound then poured antiseptic over it.

"Ow, sheesh!" Seth pulled away. "What do you have
in there? It feels like you're burning off a layer of skin."

"Chill out, Seth. I'm only cleaning the wound. You
don't want it to get infected, do you?"

"It won't get infected. This is nothing compared to
other injuries I've dealt with. Now that you've cleaned
it, I'll be fine."

"Let me check your eyes first." She squatted in front
of him.

He stared her down. "My eyes?"

"I'm checking for a concussion."

"I promise I don't have one of those either. I've
had plenty of experience in that department, too. Bike
wrecks. Construction-site injuries. You name it, I've
had it happen to me."

Caleb arrived and hurried over. "What'd I miss?"

"Cameron's ladder slipped, and Seth ran over to catch her." Josie stood looking at them, a small smile on her lips. "You saved her, Seth. That was really sweet."

"What else could I have done? Stand there and let her fall? I was the closest person to her." Seth frowned and studied the building. "How'd it happen anyway? I secured the ladder. I could have sworn it was solid when I left. How'd you get off-balance, Cam?"

"Yeah, Cam." Josie raised her eyebrows, daring Cameron to admit the truth. "How did it get off-balance?" She folded her arms and waited.

Cameron pinned Josie with her eyes. "I'm not sure, *Josie*. One minute the ladder was stable. The next it started to tip. I must have leaned to the side."

"Ya think?" Josie was on a roll. "Why'd you lean to the side?"

Cameron was ready to throttle her.

Seth walked over to check the ladder's feet. "I'm really sorry, Cam. I thought I had it secure. If something had happened to you, I would have felt awful."

Cam wanted to change the subject. "But nothing did happen. My shoulder will heal. It was my own fault. I probably should have listened when you told me not to get up there. I can be…stubborn…at times."

Seth's lips twitched.

She felt like a heel. It was her own fault. She fell because she'd been ogling Seth, but she wasn't about to tell him that. She'd never live it down. But maybe she should come clean.

She looked over at Josie. Sympathy filled her friend's eyes. She shook her head in a slight *no*.

Cameron gulped. "Anyway, don't give it another

thought, Seth. I'm fine. All's well that ends well. Right?"

"How can I not think about it? I allowed you to get hurt. And it could have been way worse."

"But it wasn't worse. The ladder barely clipped me." Her shoulder begged to differ, but he didn't need to know that. "If I remember correctly—and I do—you are the one who tried to talk me out of going up the ladder. And as I said, I've been climbing up and down ladders since I was eight years old. It was a…a fluke accident."

Josie snorted. Obvious her moment of empathy had passed.

Cameron elbowed her but kept her focus on Seth. "If you'll help me with the ladder, I'll get back up there and finish painting the trim."

"Not on my watch."

"Then I'll just finish nailing the trim for whoever's going to paint it."

"Nope."

"Oh! You're so stubborn!"

"I'm stubborn? You're the one who insisted on going up and then fell down even after I asked you not to."

"Right, I fell down on purpose, just to annoy you." She glared at him, and he stalked off with a roar. The others drifted off after him.

"Somebody has an admirer." Josie singsonged when they were alone.

"How can you say that?" Cameron turned to her. "I'm sorry, but did we just share the same experience? Because I'm pretty sure that admiration isn't a word I'd choose to describe Seth's mood right now."

Josie's laugh pealed. "He's upset because you got hurt. He's male. He lives to protect those that are weaker than him. It's conditioned into his very being. He's upset because he *likes* you. Don't you get it?"

"He doesn't like me. Not like that anyway. But regardless, it wasn't his fault. It was mine because I—" She slammed her mouth shut.

"You were checking him out. I know. I was there. Seems the two of you have a mutual admiration society going on. I've noticed it since we went to the amusement park last month."

"I'm not in the market, Josie."

"Why not? You could do worse than Seth. Far worse."

"I know. He's great. But my track record with men isn't so great. My grandpa never understood me. My husband never tried."

"Then he's an idiot, and he doesn't count. And wait—don't you mean ex-husband?"

Cameron cringed. "About that—I'm not so sure he's an ex."

"How do you figure? He left you more than a year ago. I thought he was filing for divorce."

"He did leave over a year ago, but he didn't bring up divorce until June when I told him I was moving from our home in Kansas City to here. We made that botched effort to reconcile before I came here, remember? He said he'd file, but shouldn't I have the papers by now? It's been over two months."

"Oh sweetie. That man has already put you through so much. You need to call the attorney and see what's going on." Josie glanced at Seth's retreating back. "It's time for you to make a fresh start."

"Hey man, that was quite a catch back there." Matt caught up with Seth and clapped him on the back. They fell into step and headed toward Caleb's truck. "Looks like you're going for the big leagues. I think that's awesome. I'm happy for you."

"Awesome?" Seth glanced over at Matt and shook his head. "What big leagues? I don't know what you're— oh c'mon, not you, too."

"Not 'me, too' what?" Matt's expression was all innocence.

"I didn't figure you for a matchmaker. You're a cop, for Pete's sake."

"Hey, I'm just recounting the game play. It was the stuff movies are made of."

"You've been watching too many chick flicks with Brit if that's the case. There was no game play."

"Game play? What did I miss?" Caleb rounded the truck and lifted several two-by-fours from the bed and carried them over to a small pile under a nearby tree. "I missed the local game last night, but I heard it was a good one."

"Not football, Caleb. Matt's getting in the game with Cameron."

"Matt and Cameron have a game?" Caleb grinned. "I didn't know y'all were an item."

"We aren't." Seth released the tailgate of Caleb's truck and started unloading supplies. "There is no game. And seriously, an item? You should consider spending less time hanging out with the boys from the youth group. You're starting to sound just like them."

"I'll take that as a compliment. The kids in my youth group are pretty cool." Caleb high-fived one of the teen boys.

Matt wasn't to be deterred. "Well, for all your bluster, Seth, you looked pretty cozy from my vantage point on the roof when you caught her. You held on to her for dear life after the fact." Matt started piling bundles of shingles at the edge of the tailgate. He motioned for a couple of the teen boys to come unload them. He slung a bundle of shingles over his shoulder and headed for his ladder.

"I held on to her because she was shaky," Seth called out. "I didn't want to set her down and have her collapse into a pool at my feet!"

Matt's laugh carried across the open yard.

"Not like that!" Seth cringed and glanced around the yard to make sure none of the ladies had heard him. Cameron would most definitely take the comment wrong. He'd made it sound like she was putty in his hands that melted at his touch. She might have wavered the one time before rallying—but with his arm supporting her, no one should have noticed. She'd held her own. If she showed any emotion, annoyance might be a more apt description. If anyone was shaky, it was Seth.

He shook his head. The important thing was, he'd kept a nice emotional distance from females for the better part of the past two years, and he planned to keep it that way. But when Cameron screamed, his heart had almost jumped out of his chest. He'd barely made it back around the corner in time to catch her. When he had, all he could think about was keeping her safely in his arms.

She'd felt much too pleasant there. And when she'd looked at him, her eyes all soft and doe-like, he'd forgotten about all about the people surrounding them. If Matt hadn't interrupted, Seth would have leaned in and claimed the kiss she was offering. He needed to remember to keep his distance. It didn't matter how pretty she was or how she much she caused his heart rate to increase.

He wasn't in the marketplace for romance.

Chapter 2

Josie was right. Cameron didn't plan to date in the near future, but she knew she had to take Josie's advice to follow up on the divorce. Ready to get it out of the way, she sat down to call the attorney's office first thing Monday morning when she got to work. Now, minutes later, she sat at her desk, drumming her fingers with impatience as she waited for someone at the law office to take her call.

While she was waiting, her eyes skimmed the verses of the open Bible in front of her. *"'As for me and my household, we will serve the Lord'"*.

She blinked back unexpected tears. *Lord, all I ever wanted was a marriage and family that served You. You know I never planned to divorce. But here I am. Please be with me and help me through this difficult time.*

Cameron felt better after the prayer. God had been with her through a lot of other heartaches, and He'd continue to walk with her through this. This was the final step in clearing her past and facing a fresh start.

A fresh start. The phrase reminded Cameron of a conversation she'd had with Josie shortly after their late June arrival in Lullaby.

"You're recently divorced, right? Is that why you moved here? To get a fresh start?"

Cameron nodded. "We're in the process. We didn't have a good marriage even in the best of times. Jim was a physician, and I was training in his clinic. We seemed to hit it off from the start, but even back then I should have noticed his distance and manipulative ways."

"Hey, you deliver babies, you don't analyze people," Josie said with a smile. "Even as a therapist I misread people far too often."

Cameron appreciated the empathy, though she doubted Josie had ever botched a relationship as badly as Cameron had by marrying Jim. "Well, he swept me off my feet, and I loved the attention. I guess I'm not so different than the teens in that way. I was away from family and friends. I had no time to make new friends other than the few students in my classes. We studied and worked all the time. I was lonely. Jim and I married quickly, and only after the fact did he clarify that he never wanted children." She sent Josie an incredulous look. "I mean, can you imagine? The man devotes his entire life to bringing precious baby after precious baby into the world, yet he doesn't want one of his own. I had no idea."

"The topic never came up during your counseling?" Josie asked. She made no secret about

*the fact that she wholeheartedly supported pre-
marital counseling.* "I'm guessing based on your
previous comments that you and Jim didn't take
time to get any."

"You guessed right." Cameron shrugged.
"Looking back now, I know we should have put
the brakes on, and we should have had some
counseling. Not that it would have mattered.
Jim is a master manipulator and would have
convinced the counselor and me that we'd get
through any roadblock that came our way."

"Is he a believer?"

"I'm ashamed to say he isn't." Cameron shook
her head. "Again, I saw the warning signs and
ignored them. He went to church every Sunday,
served on all the right committees—I convinced
myself that even though he didn't talk about his
spiritual life, he was one of the private types—
but it turned out his activity was all political. I
never saw any growth or love for the Lord after
we were married. He didn't live for the Lord. He
didn't live by biblical standards once we'd left the
church doors. It was all for show."

"I'm sorry." Josie said. Sympathy radiated
from her eyes. "If you ever want to talk more
about it, I'm here."

"Thank you. Trust me, there will be future issues. He left our marriage without a backward
glance. I know I'll need to talk to you about the
issues as they come up, and I'd love your insight
and advice as I deal with some of them. But not
right now." She hesitated. "Josie? For now, can
we keep my failed marriage and divorce private?

*The committee who hired us knows about it, but
I'd rather not have everyone else in town know."*

*"I would hope no one would judge you for such
a thing, but I understand how you feel. I won't say
anything. It really isn't my place. Besides, coun-
selor-client privilege, right?"*

"Right." Cameron smiled.

Cameron shook off the memory and glanced at the
clock. Her first patient of the day was due in half an
hour. She'd been on hold for the better part of five minutes and the funeral dirge music on the other end of the
line was, to say the least, grating on her nerves. She
didn't need any more reminders of the death of her
marriage. Though she had to admit the stuffy music
matched the stuffy personality of her stuffy ex-husband—or was he still her stuffy husband? Regardless,
it would figure his attorney's stuffy law firm would
follow suit.

Bored, she wondered how many other usages of
"stuffy" she could come up with before they took her
off hold. She figured she could go on and on when it
came to her ex—or non-ex—or whatever he was.

As it stood, she'd come to think of him as her ex.
He'd left her nearly a year before he actually mentioned
the word divorce. It had taken her awhile to come to
terms with the fact that she had become a statistic and
that her marriage had failed. She had been so hurt, and
so angry. But after several years of living on the edge of
his violent temper and emotional abuse, she'd only felt
relief when he stated that he'd contacted his attorney.

The divorce was in the works. Yet two long months
later, she still hadn't received the final paperwork officially ending the marriage.

Three more wasted minutes passed before a monotone voice interrupted the music. "Thank you for holding. How may I direct your call?"

"Thank heavens. I was beginning to wonder if this line really connected to anyone on the other end." She winced at her brusque words, but her nerves were stretched taut.

"Pardon?"

"Never mind. I need to talk to my husband's attorney, Fletcher James."

"Mr. James isn't in today. Would you like him to call you back?"

Cameron clenched her fist around the receiver. "No, I don't want him to call me back." She tamped down her fury. "I've been on hold for eight minutes to speak to someone who isn't even in the office? I announced that I was calling Mr. James when I was first asked to hold."

"There are several attorneys that work in this office with the last name of James, ma'am. I'm sure the person you talked to didn't know which one you referred to with your broad statement."

"I'm pretty sure *the person* I talked with was you. If there's more than one person in the firm by that name, and one was out of office, it would have been nice to have been asked *which* Mr. James I was holding for before I wasted my time." Cameron's blood pressure spiked.

The woman continued as if Cameron hadn't spoken. "Mr. Fletcher James has been out of the country for several months. Would you like for him to return your call when he returns?"

"No!" Cameron tried to collect herself. It wouldn't do to make the woman mad. *Help, Lord.* She took a deep breath. "I don't want anyone to call me back. This is Cameron Adams, and I want to speak to a human being about my husband's case, and I want to do it now. His name is Jim Reed. Surely someone can give me an update on the status of our divorce. It's been over two months."

"Just a moment, Mrs. Reed. These things take time, but I'll see if one of the other attorneys can take your call."

Before Cameron had a chance to reply, the funeral dirge returned. Another few minutes passed before a deep elderly voice filled the line.

"Hello, Mrs. Reed. Sorry to keep you waiting. Pete Blanchard. How may I be of service?"

She ignored his incorrect usage of her name. It didn't really matter as long as she received the information she sought. "I'm trying to establish the status of the Jim Reed divorce."

"Oh—you're *that* Mrs. Reed! I'm so glad you contacted us. We've been trying to reach you for months. You're a hard woman to find."

"It's Ms. Adams." She couldn't ignore it a second time. If the inept secretary had listened and announced her correctly, he'd have known her proper name.

"Pardon?"

"Cameron Adams." She tried to keep her voice even. "I've always used my maiden name professionally in my medical practice, and I plan to revert back to it in all other circumstances, too, as soon as we finish this up."

"Oh, I see. That's probably been part of the problem. We've been searching for a Cameron Reed."

Finally—some good news! If they'd been searching for her, surely that meant the divorce was final, and she was finally free of the abusive man she'd married. "Right. 'Cameron Reed' wouldn't have gotten you very far. I've moved and changed jobs since we first filed the paperwork. I'm living in temporary housing. But I did update that information with the firm at that time." She huffed out a breath. "Let's cut to the chase—you were trying to contact me to give me the final divorce papers, is that right?"

"Mrs. Reed, er, Ms. Adams. I'm not sure why you'd need the divorce papers now. Due to the circumstances, there was no divorce—it wasn't relevant. It didn't go through."

Cameron's body felt numb. She wasn't expecting *this*. "What circumstances? What do you mean, 'it didn't go through'? Jim was supposed to call you two months ago to finalize the paperwork." Cameron gritted her teeth and once again tamped down her impatience. She stared out the window at the beautiful September day, wishing she were outside enjoying the weather instead of sitting on the phone hearing depressing news she didn't want to accept.

A strange man with a clipboard walked past her office window and out of sight toward the back of the building and the lake. Distracted, she wondered if she should notify someone. With a bunch of pregnant teens in the building, they didn't need random strange men walking around the premises without clearing their presence. "Just a moment, Mr. Blanchard."

She hurried to the open doorway of her office.

Josie, her coworker, was walking down the hall.

Cameron covered the mouthpiece of the phone and motioned out back. "Someone official-looking just went across the property toward the lake. Can you check it out? I'm on the phone with the attorney."

"It's about time!" Josie smiled. "And the man you saw is the city inspector. I was just coming to tell you.

He's doing the final inspection of the building. The final step in finishing the pregnancy center! After today, Lullaby Landing should be fully ready to roll. Seth's out there with him."

Cameron's heart skipped a beat at the mention of Seth's name—but only because he'd been so kind to her. As the owner of the bed-and-breakfast inn where she was staying until she found permanent housing, he had an obligation to be kind. That was all there was to it. Josie was way off about any mutual attraction between them. From everything she'd seen, Seth was Jim's opposite in every way. He was kind, considerate, and respectful. Not just to her, but to everyone around him.

Josie smiled in amusement—probably jumping to all kinds of incorrect conclusions since Cameron had zoned out with a half smile on her face at the mention of Seth's name.

"Thanks for letting me know. Better get back to my call! I didn't see Seth out there. I mean, not that I'm watching for him or anything, but I'm sure he's around somewhere." When Josie's eyebrows rose, Cameron realized she'd protested too much. Ignoring her friend's expression, she strolled back into her office and sank down onto her black leather chair.

"I'm back, Mr. Blanchard. Sorry to keep you waiting. As I was saying, Jim was supposed to call two months ago to finalize the paperwork. And I'm sorry, while my divorce might not be relevant to you—it's very relevant to me."

"I didn't mean to offend, Ms. Adams, but in the big scheme of things, it truly isn't important. Let's retrace our conversation and discuss how the case has progressed. Maybe then I can better understand what has you so flustered. To my understanding, at the time you're referring to, sometime during the last week of June or the first week of July, Mr. Reed called Fletcher and told him you'd decided to give the marriage another try."

"It was late June." Cameron nodded, even though he couldn't see her. "That's true. We did try one last time to save our marriage. My marriage vows were very sacred to me, so I agreed to Jim's request. But within twenty-four hours we both knew we'd made a huge mistake. We'd been separated for over a year at that point. We quickly realized that nothing had changed between us. Jim promised to file the papers the following Monday morning."

The last-ditch effort to "save" their marriage had turned out to be another one of Jim's attempts to control her and the situation. He'd insisted he be the one to file—always the one to be in control. Cameron was more than happy to let him. After all, he'd been the one to bring up divorce in the first place. After their misspent weekend, he'd ordered her from the estate. She gladly moved on to her new life three hours away in Lullaby, Missouri, that very morning. She'd been waiting for the final papers ever since.

Cameron leaned an elbow on her desk and rested her head on her hand. Her stomach churned. *The divorce hadn't gone through?* What kind of game was Jim playing now?

"I'm sorry for the miscommunication, Ms. Adams, but I'm still not sure why any of this is relevant at this late date."

Cameron heard the man shuffling papers. He wasn't making sense. "Why wouldn't it be relevant?"

"Let me find your file." Mr. Blanchard sighed. "As I said, Fletcher went on vacation, but what I didn't tell you was that he then decided to retire. We've all divided his cases between us, but with full case loads of our own, it's taken awhile for everyone to get caught up."

Figures. Nothing about Cameron's marriage had been easy with Jim. Why would their divorce go smoothly? And why hadn't the secretary told her Fletcher James had retired instead of asking if she wanted him to call her back? Complete ineptness.

Mr. Blanchard's voice came back through the line. "Here we go. I have your file in my hand." She heard him page through it. "I inherited Mr. Reed's case when Mr. James retired. Once we found out about his passing, we tried hard to reach you and apprise you of the situation."

Cameron gasped. "Mr. James went on vacation, retired, then passed away? That's terrible." What an awful thing to happen. A person works his whole life, sets goals for his retirement, just to pass away before enjoying the fruits of his labor? Now she understood a bit more why things were in turmoil at the office.

"What? No!" Confusion laced the voice at the other end of the line. "Fletcher didn't pass away. I told you— he retired."

"Right... But then you mentioned his passing."

"I wasn't referring to Fletcher's passing, dear. I was referring to Jim's."

Cameron's world tilted on its axis. She felt as if someone had stolen her breath. "Is this a joke? You're talking about Jim? Jim passed *a-away*? J-Jim Reed? My husband? Why wouldn't I know this? *How* could I not know this? When did it happen?" She tried to get control of her breathing. "*What* are you talking about?"

Josie stepped into the room, her expression a mixture of shock and concern. "Cam, are you okay?"

Cameron shook her head. Josie knelt beside her, her hand resting on Cameron's noninjured shoulder. Cameron just stared at her in shock.

Mr. Blanchard's intake of breath carried across the distance. "You didn't know?"

"No. I didn't. I hadn't heard from Jim, but we had no reason to speak." She pushed her hair out of her face with a shaky hand. "How did it happen? *When* did it happen?"

"I have the date in the file." He ruffled some pages and mentioned a Monday toward the end of June.

"That's the day I left town to move down here." She exhaled. "He never made it to your office?"

"No. He didn't. I'm so sorry that you're hearing about this by phone. Do you have someone there with you?"

"Yes. My coworker—my friend—Josie is here. She's a therapist. I'll be fine. I just need to hear the details. How did he die?"

Josie's eyes widened. "Oh Cam. Do you want me to get the details for you?"

Cameron shook her head and reached up to squeeze Josie's hand.

The lawyer's voice continued on the other end of the line. "Jim hit a tree. He'd been drinking."

"I honestly didn't know. He has no family. We lived in the family home, and once I left, I never looked back."

"It's understandable under the circumstances." He cleared his throat. "But you see now why the divorce is irrelevant."

"I do, now. Yes."

"I wasn't trying to be callous."

"No, of course not."

Cameron wondered what would happen to the estate. Her grandfather had lived with her the last year she'd been in the house. She'd left his things in one of the guest rooms when she'd moved, figuring she'd send for them later.

She cleared her throat. "I'm not sure how probate works or anything, but I have some of my personal items at the house. My grandfather lived there with me this past year. He died last spring." She felt more emotion rising up at the mention of the man who'd raised her than she did at the fresh news of her husband's death. Of course, her grandfather had also been kind and thoughtful of her. "His personal items are very dear to me. Will I be able to collect them soon?"

"You can collect them anytime you please. The house and everything else in the estate belongs to you, Ms. Adams. Mr. Reed never did change his will. Everything he owned now belongs to you, including his trust."

Cameron gasped. "It does? I didn't know he ever wrote me into the will."

"Well, now you know. If I can be of any more assistance, don't hesitate to give me a call."

"Thank you." She knew when she was being dismissed.

"Let me know when you'll be in town, and we'll make plans to meet and discuss the final details of the will."

"Yes sir. It'll probably be a few weeks." Cameron hung up the phone in stunned silence.

"You okay?" Josie hadn't left her side.

"I don't know." Cameron's words felt like they were coming from far away. "Jim's dead."

"So I gathered. Cam, you're in shock. Do you want

to go lay down? We can go upstairs to my suite. Brit can reschedule your appointments."

"No, I'm fine."

"You aren't fine."

Seth chose that moment to walk past the window. His smile lit up the room, and he waved as he walked toward the lake. Cameron waved back, autopilot taking over. He didn't seem to notice anything amiss. It amazed her that someone's world could be rocked to the core while others didn't sense a thing.

"I just need a few minutes to process."

"Let me go tell Brit. She's working the front desk today. My first appointment isn't until ten. I can cover for you for a while."

Josie left the room. Moments later she returned.

Cameron shook her head. "You can't take on my midwifery patients, Josie."

"No, but I can take their vitals and get them in a room for you."

"No need." Cam sank back in her chair. "Why don't I feel more, Josie? I was married to the man for years."

"You've already grieved his loss, sweetie. Divorce, death, they're kind of the same thing. I've always personally thought divorce was harder, because there's no finality in most cases. There's always hurt for the people involved, and they have to see the other person for years—especially if the divorce involves children." Josie rubbed Cameron's arm. "And all that aside, maybe you didn't know he'd died, but from what you told me, he wasn't very nice to you during your marriage. You'd already accepted that the marriage was over. Grieving is grieving in this case, and you've had over a year to work through it."

"You really think so?"

"Yep. Death has a finality—a permanency to it. Divorce always leaves open the possibility of reconciliation, and some people cling to that hope. From what you've told me, Jim's passing will bring a healing to you that divorce wouldn't have provided."

Cameron sniffed, her eyes burning. "At least we never had any children. Thank heavens we didn't add that mistake to the rest."

"Did you want children?" Josie made no secret of the fact she longed for a big family. Her new engagement to their church's youth pastor, Caleb, gave hope that she'd soon achieve that goal.

"I do want children, but knew I'd never have them with Jim." Cameron's voice quavered, and she cleared her throat. "That final weekend, when he said he wanted to try one more time, I asked him to consider the possibility of a baby." She gripped Josie's hand. "I mean, if we were starting fresh, was it so wrong of me to bring up my desire for a child?"

"What did he say?" Josie's eyes welled.

"He stormed out of the room. But not before accusing me of trying to trap him back into the marriage by having a baby. He made it clear if I ever ended up in the family way, I'd have to 'take care of it.'"

Josie scowled. "I take it he didn't mean by raising the baby by yourself?"

"Nope."

"What happened then?"

"He told me to get out. He was filing for divorce. He locked himself in his office with his booze." Cameron squeezed her eyes shut. She hated revisiting these memories. "I got up, packed my bags, said my goodbyes, and headed here to Lullaby."

"And we're all glad you did." Josie reached over and

pulled Cam into a hug. "He made his decisions and paid the ultimate price for them."

Cameron hugged her back. "Am I weird for not feeling a desire to cry?"

"No." Josie stood and headed for the door. "Like I said, at the moment, you're in shock. Give it time. I bet when you least expect it, the tears will come."

Cameron hoped not. She felt the sadness she'd feel for any life cut short. She wished Jim's life had gone better for him. But it was hard to mourn the loss of such a mean and hurtful person. And as Josie had pointed out, she'd mourned the loss of what could have been over a year ago. "Josie?"

Josie stopped at the door and turned around. "Yes?"

"Can we keep this new development between you and me for now? The whole situation is so weird and complicated…. I'd rather kept it quiet." She huffed out a breath and tried to gather her thoughts. "I mean, people will want to show their condolences…and I don't really want them to. They might not understand. It'll be awkward."

"I understand. But you might consider telling Seth and his Aunt Ginny. They'd be hurt if you didn't let them know you were dealing with something like this."

She nodded. "Maybe in time—but not yet. I just want to mull things over on my own and find my own peace with the situation. I need to take it to prayer, try to figure out how to compartmentalize all the details. Does that make sense?" She struggled for the words to explain. "Lullaby is my refuge. I don't want Jim and our past to ruin that. Everyone knows I've recently lost my grandfather, and that's enough."

"You deserve happiness, Cam. Just don't forget that. I'm here if you need me."

Cameron analyzed Josie's words after she left. Why had she made the strange comment about happiness? Moving to Lullaby was the best thing that had happened to her since losing her parents at age eight. Maybe that was what Josie had meant. Josie didn't want this newest loss to bog her down or to steal her joy in her new beginning. She didn't intend to let it. Jim had stolen enough time and joy from her. She wouldn't let him take any more of it away through his death.

Josie had hit the nail on the head when she'd said Cameron had spent the past year working through the loss of her marriage. That's when she had truly lost Jim. And if she analyzed things really deeply, she knew she'd never really *had* Jim in the first place. Once they'd signed their marriage license, Jim had become a cold, impenetrable brick wall.

Chapter 3

"Phone for you, Cam." Ginny barely caught Cameron as she walked out the door of the bed-and-breakfast with the last load for her trip to Kansas City—a cell phone and a computer bag.

"I wonder why they didn't call my cell?" Cam hurried to the phone in the front hall.

Ginny wiped her hands on a dish towel as she stood in the kitchen doorway. "I don't know, but it sounds like one of the girls. She probably lost your card and doesn't have your number. The inn's number is listed and easy to find. You know how teens are."

"Yes, I do. I'll take it in here, Ginny. Sorry they interrupted you."

"You know I don't mind." Ginny slipped back into the kitchen, presumably to hang up the other phone.

Cameron picked up the extension. "Cameron Adams."

She had two girls close to their due dates and hoped the call wasn't from one of them saying she was in premature labor. Cameron wanted to hit the road, finalize the inheritance, and get back before she delivered the babies. She didn't like to leave town right after a birth. She preferred to stick around and make sure mama and baby were bonding and doing well. But she'd been in the business long enough to know that babies came when they were good and ready, not when it was convenient for her.

"Hey Cam." Mandy's panicked voice carried across the line. "Josie said you won't be in today because you have to go out of town."

"That's right, Mandy, but Dr. Thomas is on call to cover for me. He's a great physician and will be there for anything you need."

Mandy's voice was shaky with tears. "Nothin' personal, but I don't want Dr. Thomas! I want you to be there with me when I deliver."

"And I plan to be. I hope to be home by tomorrow night. You aren't due for a few more weeks, hon. I doubt you'll go into labor in the two days I'll be gone. Unless"—she paused for dramatic effect—"you get yourself all worked up because I'm leaving."

Seth walked into the hall and stood beside her. He whispered. "Is everything okay?"

Cameron made a face and nodded. She mouthed, "I think so."

"How can I not get myself worked up when you're leavin'?" An edge of panic in Mandy's voice made Cameron nervous. "I think I'm havin' contractions."

"I'm sure you're fine," Cameron soothed. "Would it make you feel better if I stop by the clinic before I leave town and check you out?"

"Yes. It'd make me feel a whole lot better. At least I'd know it was stress causing my contractions, not labor." She said the words with accusation, like it was all Cameron's fault that she was in a tizzy.

"It's probably Braxton-Hicks that you're feeling—practice contractions. We talked about them in class, remember?"

"I don't know, these feel pretty harsh for practice contractions."

Wait till you feel the real thing. "I'll be over in a few. I have to finish loading my car."

"So you're leaving town anyway, even though I might be in labor?"

"I promise I won't leave if we find out you're in labor. But otherwise, I have to go. How's this…. If you do go into labor when I'm gone, I'll head back immediately to be with you. I can get here in less than three hours on a weekend."

"The baby won't wait that long, will it?"

Cameron held back her sigh. Had Mandy been listening in any of their classes? "Mandy, in most cases, labor takes many more hours than that."

"You'll have your phone?"

"I'm bringing my phone. I have it right here in my hand." She waved it in the air and exchanged a smile with Seth.

"Okay. I'll see you in a few."

Cameron hung up the inn's phone. "Guess she's a bit worried about my leaving."

"Sounds like it." Seth hadn't moved.

"I'm leaving the address where I'll be staying and my cell number on this notepad." Cameron motioned to the piece of paper as she scribbled on it. "I think Ginny has my cell number, but I'll leave it here just in case." She quickly wrote the information on a sticky note while she talked. "I'll stick it here under the notepad so it won't blow away if the sticky stops working. If Mandy or any of the other girls need me, you can give them the phone number. Most of them have it, but obviously they don't always have it on hand. The address is just so someone knows where I've gone, if that's okay."

"It's fine. Actually, it's a great idea."

"I'll be right back." Cameron hurried down the entry hall toward the kitchen. "Hey Ginny, I'm heading out. I need to stop by Lullaby Landing for a few minutes before I leave town. I'll be back as soon as possible."

Ginny walked over and gave her a warm hug. "Drive carefully and be safe. I'll be praying for you."

"I will." It was nice to have someone to look out for her. "I appreciate the prayers."

Seth was waiting by the front door when Cameron returned. He followed her outside, jangling his keys as they walked. "Look, I have to run by Lullaby Landing for a few minutes myself. I have to meet with the building inspector again. I think we might have some issues with the permit. Do you want to ride along? There's no reason for us to take both vehicles when we're going to the same place."

It made more sense for Cameron to take her own car so she could leave directly from the clinic and head out. She opened her mouth to tell him, but before she could do so he smiled.

An adorable dimple that she'd never noticed creased his left cheek. Cam had a weakness for cute dimples in charming men.

"Sure, I'd love to ride along." The words popped out before she could stop them. Oh well, there was no reason to take up two parking spaces if they didn't need to. It was congested enough downtown as it was. October tourists loved the small town's shops. And if she had to admit it, she wouldn't mind a few extra minutes in Seth's company before she left town.

They reached the truck. Seth took her computer bag and phone and placed them behind the seat. She'd already loaded her purse and suitcase in her car. They'd be fine there until she got back.

He put the seat back in place and helped her up into the truck. Her waist tingled where he touched it. The interior smelled like Seth—leather and cologne. They made for a nice combination. She closed her eyes and inhaled.

Seth rounded the vehicle and climbed into the driver's seat.

Cameron looked over at him as he turned the key. "What's up with The Landing's inspection? Nothing serious, I hope?"

He put the truck in drive and followed the circular path down to the main road. "I'm not sure. We should've had the report by now, but the inspector just called and asked if I could meet with him again. He said he had a few questions and comments. I'm sure it's nothing, but I wanted to get a jump on whatever might be a problem so we could get it fixed as soon as possible."

Cameron sifted through his words in silence. "What would we do if they closed us down? Josie and Mandy have already moved in. They'd have no place to go."

Seth chuckled, the sound low and soothing. "Don't jump to conclusions. I'm sure everything's fine. We can fix anything that's out of code."

His confidence made her feel a bit better. "But what would happen to them if the city did shut us down?"

"Since we only have Josie and Mandy there, it isn't

a big deal. We'll figure something out. Don't worry about it. Okay? Between your trip back home and the girls that are due to deliver, you have enough to worry about without taking this on."

"Okay. But you'll let me know as soon as you find out?"

"I will. I promise." He turned onto Main Street. "But it sounds like you have bigger issues to deal with than I do."

"Mandy's just freaking out because I'm leaving town. You know how dramatic she can be."

"Rightfully so. I'm sure she's nervous. You and Josie are her lifelines."

"I know. And I'm sorry she's upset. But Josie isn't going anywhere. I'll try to put Mandy at ease before I leave."

"She'll be fine. I'll watch out for her until you get back." He pulled into a parking space near the clinic and hurried around to hold Cameron's door.

"Oh—she'll love that. You do know most all the girls that come through the clinic have crushes on you."

"Uh, no. I didn't know." Seth actually blushed. He looked at her out of the corner of his eye, the dimple again creasing his cheek. "In that case, maybe I should keep my distance."

"And crush their fragile spirits? I don't think so!" Cameron teased. They headed for the clinic. "It's perfectly harmless. You're the big brother they never had—or that they don't have anymore."

"I guess I can handle that." He opened the front door of the clinic for her. "I'll wait outside for the inspector. Can you let everyone know he'll be here?"

Cameron did as he asked then took the stairs two at a

time to the second level. Mandy slumped on the couch in the living area, staring mindlessly at a soap opera.

Cameron plopped down beside her. "Okay, so tell me what's going on."

"You know what's going on." A lone tear slid from Mandy's eye. Her tough-girl persona had all but disappeared. "I don't want you to leave."

"It's only for a few days. You know I'll return, right?"

"Unless something happens to you." The girl had experienced more disappointments in her short seventeen years than most people experienced in a lifetime.

"I'll be back in a couple of days. I just have some personal business to attend to. Nothing's going to happen to me, Mandy."

"You can't say that. No one knows when their time is up. At least, most people don't know."

"Your grandma knew." Cameron reached over and caressed Mandy's silky brown hair. When they'd first found her living in the woods, she'd been such a mess it was hard to tell the color of her tresses.

"Pretty much. The cancer made that known."

"Look, I know you and Josie have talked a lot about faith and trust. This is one of the situations where you need to put those lessons into practice."

Mandy's tears fell freely now.

Cameron pulled the teen into her arms. "Are you sure this is about my leaving?"

"It's about everything." Mandy sobbed. "I'm scared. I know I don't have long until the baby comes, and I don't feel like I'm ready. If you aren't here, I don't know what I'll do."

"I'm not sure any new mother feels ready when her time comes to deliver. But when it is time—and it shouldn't be for a couple more weeks at least—you're going to have a whole crew of folks wanting to help out." Cameron pulled back and squeezed Mandy's arms. "The grannies from church will elbow each other out of the way to help you with the baby. Josie and I will be right here with you. And you know Caleb and Sailor will be here, too. You have a wonderful support system in place."

Caleb and his daughter Sailor had grown close to Mandy.

"The way Josie talks, her wedding with Caleb keeps getting moved up. At the rate they're going, you might be adopted and living with them before the delivery takes place."

Mandy giggled. "I think you might be right. I can't wait for that to happen."

"Besides, I've seen your nurturing spirit. You'll be a natural at this mothering thing."

Josie exited her suite and joined them. "What did I miss?"

Cameron winked at Mandy. "Mandy's a bit nervous about my trip this weekend."

"What's up, pup?" Josie sank down on the couch on the other side of Mandy. "You know I'll be here with you."

"You don't deliver babies."

"No, but Dr. Thomas does. And even if it comes to that, I'll still be right by your side."

"What if he won't let you come in with me for the delivery?"

"Oh—he will." Cameron patted her hand. "He's great that way. And I already have the notes covering that written into your file. He has your birth plan. He knows all about you and Allie and Sailor. He's ready to see any of you if you have any problems while I'm gone."

"That makes me feel better."

"Are you still having contractions?"

"Yeah."

"Let's run downstairs and check things out."

"Okay."

Josie tagged along.

Cameron glanced over at her. "Did you get my text? I sent one a little while ago saying that Seth is meeting with the building inspector again."

"I saw that. Why did the building inspector come back?"

"I'm not really sure." Cameron shook her head and glanced over at Mandy. She didn't want the teen to have another thing to worry about. "Seth said he's sure it's nothing."

"Seth says, hmm?" Josie teased. "I noticed you rode over with him."

"You rode with him, Cam? He brought you over in his truck? Way to go!" Mandy practically gushed.

"I did, but now I'm thinking I made a mistake. I need to leave as soon as I'm finished with Mandy, and I have a feeling Seth will be awhile. I'm not even sure the inspector's shown up yet, and we're almost finished."

"I have a break between clients," Josie said. "I can run you back to your car. I need to stop by the inn anyway. Ginny said she had some treats for me, and you know I never turn those down."

"We're a mess, aren't we?" Cameron laughed. "I should have driven myself over. And if Ginny had told me she had goodies for you, I could have brought them along and saved you a trip."

"But then I wouldn't have had an excuse to go by

and say hi to Ginny. I'm sure that's why she does this. She misses my awesome presence at the inn and wants to keep me coming back. I'm sure she didn't say anything on purpose."

"I think you're right." Cameron reached over and hugged her friend. "If you don't mind giving me a ride, that'd be great. I accept."

"You two are nuts." Mandy giggled.

Cameron waved her into an exam room.

Mandy pulled Josie inside with her. Josie settled into a chair in the corner while Mandy situated herself on the examination table. Cameron wrapped a blood pressure cuff around Mandy's upper arm. They were silent as the cuff puffed tight.

Cameron watched the gauge. "Your blood pressure is awesome as usual." She put the cuff away. "Let's listen to the baby's heartbeat, shall we?"

"Yes!" Mandy settled back on the examination table and lifted the lower front of her shirt. She pushed the top of her leggings down. "I had no idea a belly could get so big."

"You aren't all that big, girl." Hearing the heartbeat was the highlight of the girls' visits to the clinic. It made the baby real to them.

Mandy's fetal heartbeat was loud and strong. "Sounds great, don't you think?"

Cameron never tired of the *swish, swish, swish* of an unborn baby's heartbeat. New life in the making. God's perfect creation. It always made her smile. "How are the contractions?"

"I haven't had another one since you asked upstairs."

"Then I think we're good to go. Promise me you won't stress while I head out of town...and I'll promise to get back to you as soon as I possibly can. Deal?"

"Deal." Mandy's response was reluctant, but the panicked look was gone.

"And do me a little favor."

Mandy wrinkled her brow. "What?"

"Maybe do a little more schoolwork and a lot less soap opera-watching? This baby is going to be here before you know it"—Cameron tapped Mandy's belly—"and the more schoolwork you get out of the way now, the less you'll have to do then."

"Oh. Good point."

"Now get back upstairs and get the books. You can work in my office while Josie runs me to the inn and returns to see her patients."

"Yes ma'am." Mandy gave Cameron a quick hug and hurried upstairs.

Seth tried to focus on the inspector's words, but he couldn't keep his thoughts from drifting to Cameron. He knew she'd be heading out soon, and he wanted to be the one to drive her home. Caleb said Seth was whipped, but Seth had denied it. The fact that his thoughts kept returning to her and that he dreaded the fact that she was leaving town told Seth otherwise. But a relationship wasn't what he was looking for. He had plenty to do with the renovations of the inn and whatever was going on with the pregnancy center. He didn't have time to chase dreams of happy-ever-after. He'd already gone down that path, and it hadn't ended well. He forced his attention back to the inspection.

So far the inspector's issues had been trivial. Seth wrote down each item as the man pointed it out, knowing the men at church could have them fixed before the end of the weekend. The inspector marked off each item they discussed on his clipboard, and he assured Seth he'd give him a copy before he left the premises.

"If you'll follow me inside, I'll show you the bigger issue."

Seth jerked his full attention back to the inspector. The way the man said it made Seth nervous. It didn't sound like the next item would be an easy fix.

"What is it?"

"I'll show you when we get upstairs."

Seth strained to think of anything that might have been shortchanged. The workmen had put forth their best efforts on the second floor living space. For most of the girls who would stay there, it would be the nicest place they'd ever lived. Seth himself had drawn up the plans, modeling the rooms after the suites at the inn. He couldn't imagine any part of the plan that would make the girls unsafe.

The man stepped into the quiet living area and swept his arms wide. "This is the problem."

Confused, Seth glanced around. "I'm not following."

"This area isn't zoned for group housing."

"It isn't exactly a group home. It's a place for individual teens to live while they're trying to get on their feet."

"Same difference in the city's eyes."

"How do you figure? Right now, we have one girl living here with a dorm mom. That isn't exactly what I consider 'group living.'"

"But the intent is for up to a dozen girls to live here at once. Correct?"

"Well, yes. In a pinch. They decided at the last board meeting that we'd probably aim for closer to half a dozen most of the time. But that was all covered when we applied for the permits."

"Half a dozen or a full dozen—it doesn't really matter. Zoning wasn't notified."

"How could we have been approved without zoning being notified? This is nuts." Seth tried to control his temper.

"I'm really sorry. I can't answer your questions. You'll have to take them up with the zoning department. In the meantime, you'll need to move out of the premises within the next couple of days."

"So if we get this taken care of within the next couple of days, we'll be good to go?"

The inspector snickered. "Uh, sure. Good luck with that. It's Friday, and we're going into the weekend. I've never seen things go that quickly, not with zoning, but one can always hope. You're run by a church group, right? Miracles do happen."

That didn't bode well. Seth could have done without the sarcasm. He bit his tongue. He wanted to get back downstairs before Cameron took off. "Is there anything else?"

"Nope, that's all for now."

It was plenty. They walked down the stairs in silence.

"Hey Seth." Mandy walked out of Cam's office and down the hall toward them, her shoulders drooping. She stopped when she drew even with them. "Cameron said to tell you she appreciated the ride over and that Josie was taking her back to the inn. Josie had to go by there anyway for something from Ginny."

Seth stopped, too. "Thanks, Mandy." He was disappointed that Cameron hadn't waited. "If it helps, I think whatever Aunt Ginny made is for both of you. You'll have some good snacks to look forward to when Josie gets back."

"Great. Your aunt makes good food." The enthusiasm didn't reach Mandy's eyes.

The inspector continued toward the front door. "See ya'll soon for the update inspection as soon as you're ready."

"We'll give you a call."

Mandy waited until the inspector closed the front door. A teasing spark lit her eyes. "If it makes you feel better, I think Cam would have rather waited to ride with you."

"Oh, you think so, huh?"

"Yep." She gave him a considering look. "Maybe you should call her and tell her you're sorry you missed her."

"So now you're a matchmaker?"

Mandy giggled.

Seth rolled his eyes. "What is it with women and matchmaking?"

"You'd be a perfect couple."

"We would, huh? And you know this how?"

"I just know. Call her and find out."

"Oh man." Seth felt his pocket for his keys and hurried toward the front door.

"Seth, what's wrong?" Mandy hurried to keep up.

"Cameron's phone. I don't think she has it. I couldn't call Cameron if I wanted to. She put her computer bag and cell phone in my truck on the way over. Did she by any chance mention stopping by to get it before she left with Josie?"

"I don't think so. They left out the back door and walked along the lake to the parking area where Josie left her car. They were deep in conversation. I doubt she gave it a thought."

"Maybe they stopped by after they got the car, but I'm pretty sure I locked the truck when we got out."

Brit, the center's director, looked up at them as they sailed past her reception desk. "Everything okay?"

"I hope so." Mandy called over her shoulder. "We're just checkin' to see if Cameron left something in Seth's car."

Seth pushed open the front door of the clinic with Mandy waddling behind him as fast as she could. He peered into the truck's window. "It's still here. I'll call Aunt Ginny and try to catch her."

He called the number, but Aunt Ginny didn't answer. He tried Josie. Still nothing. "I'll bet they're out front talking. Aunt Ginny's phone is probably lying on the kitchen counter, and Josie's is probably sitting in her car. I'd better run over there. Surely, if nothing else, I'll pass Cam on her way out of town. I can flag her down."

"She promised she'd have her phone." Panic coursed through Mandy's words. "How can I call her if she doesn't have her phone?"

"We'll get it to her, Mandy. Don't get yourself in a tizzy. I'm sure she meant well. She's just stressed about this trip, about you—she probably didn't give her phone a thought, but the minute she gets in her car I bet she'll remember."

"How can you be sure?"

"I can't be, but I'll do my best to catch her."

"What if you can't?"

"I'll get it to her." He wasn't about to set Mandy off again. "You sit tight, and I'll make sure she has her phone. Don't you go and start up those contractions again."

"I'll try not to." Mandy giggled. "Thanks, Seth. I know I can count on you."

Chapter 4

Cameron took a moment to get her bearings before she pushed open the heavy mahogany door of her former home.

Lord, I know You're here with me and that You understand how hard it is for me to go back into the house where I faced so much coldness and rejection. Please help me have the courage to get through the next couple of days—if I last that long—while I tend to my affairs. Thank You for always being there for me.

Already the dark interior was giving her the creeps. She padded into the solemn mansion and froze in the entry hall. Nothing had changed in the months since Jim's death. The word *death* still felt foreign as it rolled through her mind. She'd waited two weeks before coming back to sort through Jim's—and her grandfather's—personal items. She dreaded both tasks.

The oversized grandfather clock stood sentry over

the front hall, its ominous cadence echoing in the silence. The large antique, dwarfed by the expansive entry, still kept time, the slow tick-tick-ticking already grating on Cameron's frayed nerves.

The annoying clock had counted down many a bad moment during her years at the estate. The minutes she'd had to endure until each day would end. The minutes until the next day would begin. She could hear it from the bedroom, the kitchen, the sitting room. It tracked the minutes until Gladys would stop lecturing about decorum and position in society and how often Cameron botched everything from her party menus to hostessing. It tracked the minutes until Jim walked through the front door, always ready to let Cameron know what a disappointment she was as a wife and as a daughter-in-law. He would get irate at something as trivial as her greeting him at the door in running shorts instead of what he considered to be a proper dress.

She shook herself out of the dark memories and pressed forward into the sitting room. The dreary gray of the October weather matched her mood, filtering through wispy drapes flanked by dark, heavy curtains.

Had Gladys—her mother-in-law—still been alive, the curtains would have been drawn tight—the dark, oppressive room mirroring the woman's harsh personality.

"She isn't here, she isn't here, she isn't here," Cameron muttered, trying to dispel the ghosts in her head.

"Who isn't here, love?"

With a yelp Cameron jumped and spun in a circle, her hand against her chest. Her heart pounded beneath her open palm. Every muscle in her body tensed. Her shoulders relaxed when she looked into the kind eyes of their housekeeper.

"Eloise!" Cameron threw herself into the open arms of the only person who'd helped her stay sane while she'd lived in the house. Well, two people had helped keep her sane if she counted Eloise's husband, Alfie. After a long hug, she pulled back and put a hand against her still pounding chest. "You scared the bejeebies out of me, sneaking up like that."

"Wasn't no sneakin' goin' on from my end." Eloise laughed, the corners of her eyes crinkling her mahogany skin. Smooth white hair framed her face, pulled back in a perfect bun. "I walked in here plain as day as soon as I heard that front door slam shut. I knowed it was you comin' home, and I wanted to snatch my first hug."

"I missed you, too." Cameron hadn't realized how much until just now. She felt bad for not keeping in touch, but she figured she'd lost the privilege of a relationship with Eloise and Alfie when Jim ordered her out of the house in June. Her world tilted a bit more upright now that Eloise was in the room with her. She looked over Eloise's shoulder. "Where's Alfie?"

"Oh, you know him. He's outside—putterin' around on the grounds somewhere. He's always lookin' for somethin' to do."

"I'll have to hunt him down before I leave again."

Eloise's face fell. "You ain't stayin' around a bit? We been missin' you somethin' fierce. This old place is hardly bearable since you been gone."

The guilt pinged again. She'd left the area without a backward glance, but Eloise and Alfie had been stuck there. She hated seeing the disappointment in Eloise's eyes. The woman had been the closest thing to a grandma she'd ever had. The closest thing to a mother figure, too. "I'm sorry, El, but I have to get back to my new job. I have several girls due to give birth, and they need me there."

"I s'pose they do. You do your job so well. We were both so excited to hear from you when you called last month to say you were comin' home—even if you're only here for a short visit. As I said, it's been real lonely."

"I can imagine." Cameron suppressed a shudder of revulsion. Words could never express how happy she'd been to walk out those doors to start her new life. Eloise and Alfie had been left behind, alone, to run the big place. "I should have called sooner. Jim made it clear you'd lose your job if I tried to contact you. As I told you on the phone, I didn't even know about his passing until a couple of weeks ago."

"I understand, girlie. If I'd been in your shoes, I'd have done the same thing. I'd have taken the opportunity and run with it and never looked back. Stayin' on here ain't been nothin' but lonely."

Cameron understood lonely. Her grandfather had taken over as her legal guardian after a house fire claimed the lives of her parents. All their meager belongings had burned with them. Cameron had been eight. Her grandfather had tried hard, but he was a widower and set in his ways. For the most part, Cameron had figured out how to entertain herself while trying not to be underfoot. It made for a very lonely existence.

"I truly am sorry, El." She didn't know what else to say. She didn't have an alternative. Eloise and Alfie had been a part of this estate since Cameron's deceased husband was a baby—surely they wouldn't want to leave the only home they'd had for half a century. They were well past retirement age.

"Have you made any decisions about the house?" Eloise asked, as if reading Cameron's mind.

"Decisions?" Cameron looked at her, confused. "Not really. I mean, I knew I had to come up here and go through some things. The long weekend gave me the opportunity to do that."

"But you're only stayin' a day?"

Cameron had originally planned to stay through Monday, but the eerie house was already taking a toll. "I can possibly stay longer. Do you think it'll take that much time to sort through the belongings? I scheduled an appraisal for the antiques before I came up here. No reason to leave them sitting around. I just met with the attorney, so I have that out of the way."

Eloise dusted her hands on her apron. "Now you know me, chile—don't wanna speak ill of the dead or nothin', but I've already packed up the old bat's belongin's, knowin' you wouldn't be partial to the job. I know how hard you tried to get along with the old biddy during the three long years before your marriage met its demise, but she made it impossible. Then her son wouldn't hear of you or me packin' up her things when she was gone. Oh, goodness no. We had to leave them as they were. If'n you ask me—he left her things there with hopes that they'd haunt us all. She might not be here, but her tainted stuff sure is. You know?"

"Eloise!" Cameron choked on her laugh. "You know better than that."

"I certainly do. The good Lord don't allow no such goin's on, but I'm sure that's what that husband of yours hoped would happen. Not meanin' any disrespect towards the dead or anythin', but the minute I heard about that dirty rottin' good for nothin' deadbeat's passin', I packed up his mama's stuff and put it away."

The chatty woman never missed a chance to speak her mind.

"Oh thank heavens, Eloise! Bless you. I've dreaded that job."

"I know you did, honey. It's all done and over with, and the boxes are in the garage, awaitin' your direction. I can call someone to come pick them up if you decide you want to donate. I put anythin' that looked of value in a separate box in her quarters for you to look at."

Cameron waved her hand. "Donate. Please. Get rid of the things." She grinned. "I don't want to speak ill of the dead either, but hopefully those belongings will find a much nicer owner in their new homes."

"Can't find much worse than they had here." Eloise nodded. "That woman treated her belongin's better'n she treated you. Wasn't right a'tall." She hesitated and peeked up at Cam through lowered lashes. Guilt washed over her features.

"Out with it, El. You know I could never be angry with you. What else do I need to know?"

"Nothin' bad, I hope. I done did the same thing with the mister's clothes. I packed 'em up and stuffed the boxes in the garage. I raised that boy better, but his mama was a powerful mess, and apparently her influence took. That man and his mama was nothin' but nasty to you, and you deserved better."

Eloise raised her chin a notch, daring Cameron to care. She didn't. If she never saw her husband's clothes again, it would be too soon. "The only thing I'd have done different is to burn them so I'd never have to see anyone wearing his 'custom' originals anywhere near me."

"Bless someone else with his things. Make the ridiculous expense he put into all them clothes count for somethin' good. Since you're three hours south of here, I don't think you'll have to worry about seein' them. Besides, it sounds like you runnin' in a whole different crowd down there in Lullaby than you ran with here. Sounds heavenly." Her face creased into dimples and a soft smile.

"It is a different world down there, Eloise. You'd love it. Slow paced. Everyone cares about everyone else. I've already made some good friends." A sense of peace filled Cameron. "You don't know how happy I am to hear that you've already done all the packing. I've dreaded this trip for nothing."

"You dreaded the trip even with Al and I on the other end waitin' for your visit?" Eloise asked.

Cam hugged her again. "Oh El. I didn't dread that part of the trip. I'd never dread a visit with you. I just dreaded the going-through-things part."

"You should've asked. I'd've put your mind to ease. You had to have known I'd be more than willin' to box the things up for you."

"Obviously—since you already did!" A heavy weight had lifted from Cameron. "But I didn't want to pawn the job off on you. It was my mess to deal with."

"Takin' care of those you love is what family is all about, darlin'. It's high time you learned that. I know you haven't had much experience with havin' folks care, but your grandpa did his best, and you know Al and I love you like you're our own kin. You're all the family Alfie and I have in this world."

Tears filled Cameron's eyes. "I've never had someone say anything like that to me."

"It's high time you did." She hooked Cameron's arm with her own. "Let's go find that man of mine, and you can give him a quick squeeze before we send him out for your bags. All the grunt work is over and done, so you can spend some time with us before you head back."

"I still have to go through my grandfather's things, but that'll be quick work. He didn't believe in having excess material goods."

"Your grandfather had the right idea. Al and I live with the same philosophy."

They walked down the wide hall and entered the large kitchen. The kitchen was Eloise's sanctuary, and she'd insisted on making it her own. The room shone with her charm, from the lavender wallpaper to the bright splashes of green and white that complemented the décor. Living green plants rested on every surface, giving life to the oppressive mansion.

The kitchen was the only room where Cameron had felt the gloominess of the house fall away. Whether because of Eloise's cheerful presence, the room's brightness, or both, it was her refuge as long as she'd lived there. Where Jim and Gladys always found fault with her, Eloise and Alfie always had a kind, positive word to pick her up.

They passed through the kitchen and out onto the large back porch. The trees were starting to change with the coming of autumn, but the grass was still a brilliant green. Beautiful plants surrounded the circumference of the patio.

"It's gorgeous, as always. Alfie does such great work on the lawn and gardens."

"This always was your favorite place to escape."

"I could breathe out here, at least until one of them chased me down to remind me of my many failings."

"Honey chile, you had no failin's. Their problems were all of their own makin'."

"I know, but—"

"Am I seein' things, or has our prodigal daughter come home?" Alfie's deep, rumbling voice carried to Cameron from the far side of the bushes.

"You're seeing things, Alfie." Cameron laughed. "I'm a vision from your imagination."

"You're a vision all right. And a good one, at that!" He rounded the bushes and pulled her into a bear hug.

Tears threatened at his kind words.

Cameron remembered the time Jim had walked out in time to see Alfie swing her into one of his exuberant hugs. Jim had chastised her for her lack of decorum. He'd lashed out at her for "fraternizing with the hired hands." His own nanny—who'd loved him dearly—and her husband had been relegated to "hired hands." The memory had her hugging Alfie back with a teary embrace. "I've missed you."

"I've missed you, too, little girl."

"How long are you going to call me that?" Cameron laughed as she wiped at her eyes. "I'm only a few credits short of getting my doctorate. I have my master's in nursing, you know."

"Oh I know, all right. How could I forget my only daughter's hard-sought achievements?"

Cameron's heart warmed.

"You usin' that degree?"

"I am. I love my job in Lullaby. I've been working at the hospital up until lately. My backup doctor has been very accepting of me. The patients are wonderful, too. Now I'm starting to see more patients at our clinic. I love it."

"I'm happy to hear it. Any baby would be blessed to see your smilin' face first thing after he or she arrives in this world. And you deserve to be happy. You deserve so much better'n what you've had." His words echoed Josie's.

"Thank you, Alfie. I've sure missed you both."

The doorbell rang from the front of the house.

"Lord have mercy. It's grand central station around here! No visitors for months, then everyone comes at once." Eloise hurried toward the door. "I'll see who's here, and then I'll bring dinner out to the patio. You two sit and visit."

Alfie pulled a chair for Cameron. She sank onto it. The drive had been long, and she should be ready to walk or work, but her emotions were shot. She'd lost time by meeting with Mandy, stopped for lunch, driven the three hours to town, hit rush hour traffic, and met with the attorney. It all made for a long day. "You've kept the place looking nice, Al."

"Glad to hear you think so." He grinned. "Especially since you're the new owner. What do you think of that? I've taken some liberties with the garden. Things I've always wanted to do, but the tyrant and her spawn never would let me do them. Hope you don't mind."

"Mind? Me? Why would I care?" Cameron laughed.

"This place is yours of course." Alfie scowled. "Not sure that's a great thing after all the torment you endured here."

"It wasn't the happiest time of my life." Those years had disappeared when she was eight. "But they weren't the most awful either. I got by."

"Gettin' by isn't livin', hon. You deserve more than to just 'get by.' "

"I suppose so." She looked out over the acreage. "I guess I hadn't thought about the inheritance much. I haven't ever thought of this place as my own."

"Well, you better start thinkin'." Alfie laughed.

"Most people would give their right arms to own a place like this. You inherit and don't even think about it. You are truly one of a kind."

She gave him a wry grin. "Guess that proves my dear mother-in-law wrong. She always thought me to be a gold digger, marrying her son just to steal away his riches."

"That's because she couldn't imagine any other reason why someone would want to marry the clod." His eyes widened. "I'm sorry—I didn't mean that as an insult toward you...."

She waved him off. "I understand. I look back, and even I can't explain why I married him."

"I can." He placed his dark, work-worn hand on top of hers. "You were lonely and had a lot in common with him. He could pour on the charm when he wanted to. If only Eloise and I had known you better back then, we could have warned you off."

"Would you have? Warned me off? I mean—if we'd had time to build a friendship when we first met?"

He stared into the distance for a long minute. "I don't know. I'd like to think I would have."

"If it makes you feel better, I doubt I'd have listened. I didn't know you all that well back then. Jim made sure to keep me far away from y'all. And even if I had been warned off, we'd have never gotten to know each other, and we wouldn't have this bond. That alone is worth it to me, Al."

His eyes grew moist. "Those are some kind words to warm an old man's heart." He patted his chest with his large hand.

"I mean them."

"I know you do."

The back door opened, and they turned to see Eloise

leading Seth out onto the porch. Deep dimples creased both his cheeks when his brilliant blue-green eyes settled on Cameron.

"Seth?" Flustered, Cameron jumped to her feet. "Is everything okay back home? Did something happen to Ginny or one of the girls?"

"Everything's fine." He smiled. "You left your phone and a small bag behind. Mandy panicked."

"Oh no! And you had to drive them all the way up here? I knew I'd left my phone, but by the time I realized it, I'd come too far to turn around. I felt awful after I promised Mandy I'd have it with me at all times. I was going to call her with the estate's number as soon as I arrived, but I got caught up in visiting." She took a deep breath. "I'm rambling. I'm so sorry you had to drive it all the way up here. How could I be so careless?"

"You have a lot on your mind." Seth joined them at the table. "Aunt Ginny was worried about you driving all this way and back and not having a phone. She wanted me to trace your path and make sure you made it safely…and to give you your things. You know how she is. And Mandy, as I said, was panicked. I promised her I'd get it to you. I figured you'd need the computer to finalize details of your grandfather's estate."

Cameron knew she'd led him to believe it was her grandfather's estate, and she didn't correct him. She didn't see why it mattered. She hoped Eloise and Alfie would keep quiet about the details, too. They were private people, and well versed in discretion, so she couldn't imagine a reason for them to speak of her deceased husband or mother-in-law while Seth was here.

Both of them looked at her with curiosity. She gave a short shake of her head.

Alfie grinned at Seth then Cameron as he watched

their interaction. He and Eloise exchanged a warm glance. "Care to introduce us to your *friend*, Cameron?"

Seth didn't miss Alfie's emphasis on *friend* and neither did Cameron. Seth ducked his head to hide his smile.

"Seth owns the bed-and-breakfast inn where I'm staying."

"Mm-hmm. Is that so?" Eloise folded her arms over her ample bosom and looked him over.

"Yes'm." To Seth's credit, he stood tall and let Eloise peruse him.

Alfie motioned for Seth to pull up a chair. A roll of thunder in the distance saved the moment. Alfie hurried to his feet. "Oh, goodness. In all the excitement of Cameron comin' home, I plumb forgot about those storms that are comin' through this evenin'."

"Storms?" Cameron hated thunderstorms, especially in this huge old creaky house. She wished again that she hadn't come. Eloise and Alfie were wonderful, but the house… She wished she were on the sunny back deck of the inn, lakeside, sharing a cozy dinner with Ginny and Seth. And she wished she could take Eloise and Alfie with her.

Chapter 5

"Hey Aunt Ginny. I just wanted to let you know I arrived at Cameron's place, and she made it here just fine, even without her phone."

"Oh, thank the Lord, Seth. I'm so glad to hear it. I've been worried. I don't know how we ever traveled before the use of cell phones."

Seth laughed. "I guess back then we had to focus on faith instead of technology."

"I still focus on my faith, young man. And don't you ever think otherwise!"

"Of course you do. You know I'm teasing."

"You aren't heading back home tonight are you?" Aunt Ginny's anxiety carried across the miles.

"I am. I plan to head back as soon as we finish eating. I've been invited to dinner by Cameron's housekeeper."

"Housekeeper? Cameron has a housekeeper? I would

never have known. She's always so down to earth and low-key. She does for herself. She's never expected to be waited on, even when I've tried to wait on her."

"I know, and I agree. I was pretty surprised myself." Seth glanced over at Cameron. She hadn't seemed the wealthy type to him either. When he'd arrived, the sheer immensity of the mansion had him stopping in the middle of the road to make sure he'd put the proper address in the GPS. Her car sitting in front of the house at the end of the winding drive removed any doubt.

"She never puts on airs." Aunt Ginny sighed. "The world needs more people like her."

Seth studied Cameron as she worked alongside Eloise to secure the items on the deck. She worked every bit as hard as her employee. As a matter of fact, he'd heard her suggest several times that the older woman sit down and take a load off. He walked to the far side of the patio while he talked and finished securing the items on his side. "Well, Auntie, it just goes to show, life always holds surprises. People aren't ever what we think they are—whether good or bad."

"Now Seth, I know where you're going with this. Don't you be judging Cameron by Sylvia's bad choices."

"I'm not judging her at all. I'm just saying no one is as they appear to be. Cameron is a perfect example of that. People in general aren't what they seem like on the surface, once you get to know them."

"Most people are exactly what they appear to be. I never thought you'd grow up to be so cynical." Aunt Ginny sighed. "I know Sylvia hurt you, Seth, but most people aren't like her. There were signs. You just chose not to see them. I've seen nothing but good in Cameron."

"I met with the building inspector today."

"I see. So we're changing the subject? Before you do, I have one more thing to say. Just give Cameron a chance—that's all I ask. She's a good person. I know she is. I never felt that way about Sylvia. There was always something—"

"I hear what you're saying, Auntie," Seth interrupted. "Now, as I was saying, I met with the inspector, and he gave me bad news. I didn't have a chance to tell you earlier—I was in such a hurry to catch Cam before she got out of town. Aunt Ginny—they're closing down the center."

"What?" she sputtered. "They can't do that. We've hardly had a chance to open. Why on earth would they close it down? We have appointments to keep. Babies on the way. The girls are involved in their weekly meetings. The city can't take that away from the girls at this point."

"They can, and they are."

"What exactly is the problem?"

He glanced over at Cameron. She and Eloise had their heads together, laughing. He didn't want to ruin Cam's weekend. She had enough to worry about. He lowered his voice. "The inspector said the second floor wasn't cleared for group living."

"That's his problem? It's just a few teen girls."

"You know that. I know that. But the inspector doesn't seem to care. Ordinances are ordinances."

"So we need to make some phone calls."

"Apparently. For starters." Seth rubbed a hand across his face. "We'll have to meet with the city. You might call some of the men from church that have connections, ask them what we'll need to do to get the ball rolling."

"I can do that. I'll get on it right away."

Seth could envision the gears turning in her head.

"In the meantime, I have the perfect solution," she said. "We can have the girls stay here at the inn until we get things straightened out."

"Excuse me?"

"You heard me. We have the room. We don't need the income. We've invested well. We can get by for a while without filling all the rooms with paying guests. We're pretty much closed to paying guests for renovations anyway."

"No, Aunt Ginny. Renovations and sleeping babies won't mix. And all those teenage girls running around? No way. It'd be like having a houseful of Sylvias. I haven't minded helping with the clinic. I've donated a lot of man-hours to getting the building up and running. I designed the plans. But an inn full of raging, post-pregnancy hormones? I draw the line there."

"They aren't like Sylvia, Seth! You have to get past that. These are young girls who have a lot on their plates. You have no idea what their stories are. You do know Mandy's story. Does she resemble Sylvia in any way?"

She had him there.

"No." Seth bit the word out between clenched teeth. "She was a lonely, hurting girl who was looking for love in the wrong place."

"Exactly. Sylvia wasn't lonely, she wasn't hurting, and she wasn't young. She was calculating and conniving. None of the girls in the program are anything like her."

Seth contemplated her words. "You're right." He pushed his hair back from his face with a growl.

Cameron glanced over at him, her eyes questioning.

"Inn issues, Cam. Nothing major." He shook his head

and waved her away. He returned his attention to his conversation with his aunt. "I guess they can have the third floor."

"That's a perfect idea! Seth—I knew you'd do the right thing."

"You'll need to notify Josie. I haven't spoken to her yet. Let her know about the ruling and about the new plans. Tell her to leave the large things like furniture at the center—to just bring what they need for a short stay. I don't expect this to take long, and even if it does, they can grab more things later."

Thinking they were finished with the conversation, Seth walked back over to the patio table and sat down.

"So, Seth, back to your plans for the evening..."

"I still plan to head out after dinner, Aunt Ginny."

Cameron shook her head. Seth raised his eyebrows in question.

Aunt Ginny distracted him. "You can't leave this late. Not after all that driving you already did to get there. It's getting dark, and I saw on the Internet that your area is expecting storms to move through. They expect them to be severe."

A roll of thunder underscored her comment.

"I'll be fine, Aunt Ginny. I'll take my time, and I'll drive carefully. You know I'll be okay."

Cameron motioned for him to wait.

"Hang on. Cam's trying to tell me something."

Cam walked over and sat down beside him. "You can't drive all the way back tonight. That would be insane. There's a storm. We have plenty of room here at the house. You can spend the night and head out fresh in the morning."

Seth covered the mouthpiece with his thumb. "That's not necessary. As I told Aunt Ginny, I'll be fine."

"Seth? You listen to that girl." Aunt Ginny's voice blared through the phone.

He must have hit the speakerphone button by accident.

Cameron laughed. "Aunt Ginny has spoken. You don't want her to be up late worrying, do you?"

"She's right, Seth. Did you hear her? And I will worry."

"If you heard her, Aunt Ginny, I think you know that I did, too." He rolled his eyes.

Cameron's blue eyes twinkled. "We'll keep him here with us, Ginny, and make sure he's safe. Thanks so much for everything!"

"Thank you, darlin'," Aunt Ginny gushed. "You two have a good evening."

"Bye, Aunt Ginny." Seth knew better than to argue when both women were teaming up against him.

He glanced over at Eloise.

Her head bobbed in agreement. "Good choice, son. This won't be a night for you to be caught out on the road."

Seth watched as Alfie hurried toward a shed with an armload of tools. "I better head out there and make myself useful if I'm staying."

He left the women and hurried in the direction where Alfie had disappeared.

"That's one good-lookin' fella, Cameron. I see now why you didn't come home sooner." Eloise reached for Cameron's hand and pulled her from the table. "Let's rustle up dinner for the men. They'll be mighty hungry when they get inside."

Cameron followed her friend inside. "What all needs to be done out there? I can help, too."

"Nonsense—though I'd want to be trailin' that good-lookin' honey, too, if I were you. But the truth is, you'll be a much better help to me in here. We need to have things ready in case the electricity goes out. Seth seems to be a hard worker. He did a great job helpin' us secure the patio plants and decorations. The men just have to stow the equipment Al was usin' before you showed up, and they'll need to secure the lawn furniture in case the winds start blowin'." She glanced out the window. "Which it already seems to be doin'."

Cameron shuddered. "I hate storms."

"I know, dear. I remember. All the more reason for you to stay in the house." She pointed toward the wall on the far side of the table. "Why don't you pick out some pretty candles from the china cabinet over there? A festive dinner table will give you a fresh frame of mind."

Cameron raised her eyebrows. "Are you trying to set a mood?"

Eloise's expression was one of pure innocence. "Who, me? I'm just thinkin' ahead. If the electricity goes out, we'll be in total darkness."

"We have a whole-house generator if that's the case."

"It takes time to kick in." Eloise peeked out of the corner of her eye at Cameron. Her brown eyes twinkled. "Besides, a little ambience never hurt anyone. It might just put your nerves to rest."

"My nerves are just fine, thank you very much." Thunder crashed, and Cameron yelped. With a fleeting look toward Eloise, Cam headed over to collect the candles. She had to admit the warmth and glow would calm her nerves, whether she wanted to admit it to Eloise or not. But a candlelight dinner with Seth put her nerves on edge more than the storm did.

Lightning flashed, and thunder boomed. She wished the men would hurry up and return.

"Storm's movin' closer." Eloise pulled food from the refrigerator. "If you don't mind, we'll eat some of the brisket Al cooked up this morning. I'm afraid anything else will get caught in the oven if we have a power outage."

"Brisket sounds delicious." Cameron's mouth watered. "Did Alfie cook it in the smoker?"

"He sure did. As soon as you mentioned you were comin', we made a list of your favorite foods. I have baked beans, a garden salad, and homemade bread to go along with it."

"You're trying to entice me to move home for good."

"Is it workin'?"

"No, but maybe I'll take you back with me."

Hope lit Eloise's eyes for a moment, then the emotion dimmed. "Now you're just teasin' me."

Cameron grabbed the opportunity. "You'd be willing to come back to Lullaby with me?"

"I'd leave this place and follow you to that dream town in a heartbeat. Didn't I say we've missed you somethin' awful?"

"Well, yes, but I didn't think you missed me enough to move to Lullaby. If you're serious, this is something we need to discuss." Hope flamed inside Cameron. "I'd love to have you and Alfie in Lullaby!"

"You seem surprised by the thought. You didn't think we'd want to move closer to you? It's not like we have a lot of options when it comes to movin'. We've saved a nice nest egg over the years, but we have no children, no kin, no one other than you. Where else would we go?"

"I thought you'd want to stay here at the estate. You've been here for years. It's your home."

"And we figured you'd want to sell it."

"I would never sell your only home!"

Eloise joined her at the table. She placed her weathered hand on Cameron's, much like Alfie had done earlier. "We're ready to slow down, Cameron. This estate takes a lot of work. And it's silly to leave this huge place sittin' empty when you can invest the money from its sale elsewhere."

"Oh Eloise. I never gave a thought to how hard you have to work to keep this place going. I figured with all of us out of the way you'd be able to relax and enjoy your retirement. I'm sorry for being so thoughtless."

"You didn't know. But now that you do, what are we goin' to do about it?"

"I know for starters we're going to put this house on the market, and I'll figure out a way to move you down to live in Lullaby with me."

Lightning flashed, closer this time.

Cameron jumped. "Are you sure I shouldn't go out and help? The sooner we get things put away, the sooner everyone will be safe inside."

"You think I'm gonna send you out on a night like this? You're jumpin' like a cat on a hot tin roof. Alfie knows how much you hate these storms. If you go out there, he'll likely send you right back in. If he doesn't, he'll worry. Either way, you'll just slow them down."

"And Seth will complain about my being out there, too. He gets all manly on me when I try to do too much."

"Good for him!" Eloise laughed. "That boy is a good catch, one you'd best not let go."

"Have to have him on the line before he's a good catch, El. Can't let him go if he isn't hooked."

"Oh, from what I've seen, you have that boy hook, line, and sinker. You might not know it. He might not know it. But I know bloomin' love when I see it. A person doesn't chase all over the state to deliver a phone and a bag just for the fun of it."

"He knew it was important to one of the girls that she be able to reach me, El. Don't read anything more into it."

"I seen how he looks at you, too. When he thinks you aren't watchin', he studies you. Mm-hmm." She raised her nose a bit higher in the air. "I'm tellin' you. I know love when I see it, and love's written all over that one's face. If you look in a mirror, you'd see it on your face when he's around, too."

"I'm not looking anywhere. If you'll think a minute, you'll remember I just got out of a bad marriage. I'm not looking to start dating again."

"Sometimes love don't give you a choice, honey chile. And that marriage has been over for a year now."

"Doesn't feel like it to me."

"That's because you had that blip when you mistakenly thought you should give it one more go, based on his ridiculous beggin'. But from where I stand, you've been alone for far longer than a year. That husband of yours ignored you the better part of your marriage."

The back door swung open, and Seth and Alfie hurried inside. Cameron couldn't be happier at the interruption. She knew Eloise was right, but she needed time to put her tumultuous emotions to rest.

"You boys stay right where you are and let me grab some towels. I won't have you drippin' all over this fine floor."

Cameron hid a smile. The tiles would hardly be affected by a little rainwater. Seth did as told, his amused expression mirroring Cameron's thoughts. Alfie stood stoically by the door, his expression one of timeworn lessons learned.

"Here ya go. I should have had these towels waitin' at the door for you." She busied herself with drying Al's hair and clothes while glaring and motioning with her head for Cameron to do the same for Seth.

Horrified, Cameron shook her head no.

Seth made quick work of the task and pushed his long hair away from his face. He walked over to sit next to Cameron. "Something smells good in here."

"It's probably Cameron. She's a sweet-smellin' thing, don't you agree?" Eloise waggled her eyebrows.

"El!" Cameron couldn't believe her friend's audacity.

"You have a point." Seth leaned close and breathed deeply. He lowered his voice. "Are you wearing barbecue tonight, Cam? It smells so good it's making my mouth water."

"Lots of things smell good." Cameron's face felt like it was on fire. She discreetly tried to scoot her chair farther away, but the chair leg was stuck against the table's leg. "Eloise and Alfie made my favorite—smoked brisket—along with all my favorite sides."

Seth hooked a finger under her chair and pulled her closer to him.

Darn, he hadn't missed the maneuver.

"Ah, they spoil you."

Cameron laughed out loud. "Just like Ginny spoils you?"

"What? She cooks nice things for the inn, and I'm blessed to be able to benefit from that."

"Aren't we all? Listen, speaking of the inn, El and I were talking, and she said they'd be willing to move to Lullaby."

"Really?" Seth reached over and squeezed Cameron's hand.

Eloise's and Alfie's touches had brought familiar warmth, but Seth's touch sent shivers running up her arm.

"That's great. I bet you'll love having them there."

"I—I will." Seth's nearness made it hard to concentrate. "It would be nice to have family around. They're the closest thing I have left."

Across the kitchen, Eloise was telling Al to get into dry clothes.

Seth watched with interest. "She reminds me of Aunt Ginny. They're certainly cut from the same cloth. I think they'd get along well."

"Yeah. I think you're right."

"You've grown distant. What's on your mind?"

"I have so much to do. I'll need to find a house before I can bring Alfie and El down to Lullaby. I need to go through my grandfather's things and pack them up. And I need to put the house on the market."

"I can help you with that." Eloise opened a few drawers before she found what she was looking for. "Here we go. A neighbor came by a few weeks after Jim passed away, asking if we planned to sell."

"Your grandfather's name was Jim?"

Cameron side-stepped Seth's question. "What did you tell him?"

Eloise hesitated, glancing between Seth and Cameron. "I said I wasn't sure, so he left the card, asking that he be contacted before we listed the place. He was a nice man. I told him I'd leave the card in the drawer until we made a decision."

"I guess I'll call him tomorrow."

Seth played with his napkin. "You'll still want to

get an appraisal. Do you know anyone who can come by on short notice?"

"I think so. A lady at church started selling houses after her husband left her. She's done really well. I'll make that call after dinner. It would be nice to have things settled in the morning."

"If you can finish things up, we can head back to Lullaby together."

"I'd like that." She hoped she didn't sound desperate. "Safety in numbers and all."

Al returned to the kitchen, and Eloise brought the platters of food to the table.

"Look at you, Eloise! Here I sat and chatted away while you did all the work. I'm so sorry."

"Nonsense. I already had the salad on a platter. I just had to pull off the plastic wrap. The bread was waiting in the basket. We'll slice it at the table." She placed a floral ceramic butter crock and matching serving knife beside the basket. "And I warmed the baked beans in the microwave. They were cooked and flavored earlier in the day." She perused the layout. "Like I said, a nice, easy dinner."

The storm raged outside the window and knocked the power out midway through the meal. Cameron's gasp must have clued Seth in to her discomfort. He reached for her hand and squeezed it under the table.

"Thanks," she whispered. His hand felt strong and warm in hers. She clung to it a moment, then forced herself to let him go.

He wiped his mouth with his napkin and settled back in his chair. "That was some fine cooking, Eloise. You'd give my Aunt Ginny a run for her money in the kitchen."

"Just for that, you can have a double helping of dessert." Eloise lifted a serving spatula full of blueberry cobbler onto his plate.

Alfie grunted. "Hey now. I braved that storm along with Seth, and I compliment your cookin' all the time." Alfie held his plate out.

Eloise sent him a loving glance and cut him a large serving, too.

Cameron's eyes misted. She could only imagine what it would be like to have a husband who showed his love so clearly. She glanced over at Seth, and he winked. He'd be the type to show his affections. Cameron blushed and quickly looked away. "As much as I love your baking, El, I'll take a small helping. I'm not sure I can find space for anything more."

Alfie took a large bite. "So, if you don't mind my askin', how's the clinic comin' along?"

"It's doing great." Cameron smiled. "Our first girl moved in, and we have a couple others in the registration process."

"About that, Cam." Seth reached for her hand again. "I met with the inspector before I came here."

"Oh! I forgot all about that meeting. How did it turn out?" Seth had her full attention.

"I hate to tell you this, but they're closing us down."

Cameron's stomach lurched.

He put his hand up, motioning for her to wait and let him have his say. "But I don't think it'll be for long."

"How can they do this? Why now?"

"They said we weren't licensed for a group situation. Somehow code and zoning had a mix-up in communication."

She shook her head, trying to take it in. "This is huge, Seth."

"No, it isn't. We can still use the clinic for meeting patients. Nothing has changed there."

"But what about Mandy and Josie? What about other girls who will need a place to stay?"

"I talked to Aunt Ginny. She's convinced me to open up the third floor of the inn to anyone who needs the pregnancy center's help. We can handle the same amount of girls, if not more. And we are approved for group living."

Eloise clapped her hands together. "That's a wonderful thing to do, Seth." Her smile faded. "But it sounds like a bad time for Al and I to move down there. We wouldn't want to burden you more than you already are."

Cameron shook her head. "Eloise, you'll never be a burden to me, and you know it! You might as well start packing your boxes tonight. I'm taking you home with me. We just need to find us a house and get you moved in."

"We have plenty of room at the inn, Cam," Seth said. "Your family is more than welcome to stay there with us. There's no need to rush into buying a house before you're ready."

Seth's words were casual, but something in his eyes begged her to stay at the inn. No way could she tell him no.

Chapter 6

Saturday morning dawned sunny and clear. The storm from the previous evening had moved through, leaving nothing but downed branches and leaves in its wake.

Cameron decided to go on an early morning run before they started their workday. Even with the storm, she'd managed a good night's sleep. She suspected it had something to do with Seth staying at the house. His presence made her feel safe.

She'd set a nice pace when a neighbor waved her down.

"Hi, Mrs. Reed."

Cameron gritted her teeth. She'd never met the neighbor. It wasn't his fault he didn't know she went by Adams. "Hi."

"I just wanted to say how sorry my wife and I are for your loss. Your husband was a good man. He delivered all three of our children before he went into teaching. My wife adored him."

"Thanks." Cameron resumed jogging, and the man kept pace in his car. She never was sure what to say to a comment like that. The man the neighbor thought he'd known wasn't the man she'd known.

"I gave your housekeeper my card. My wife has had her eye on your place for years, and we'd love to buy it if you decide to sell."

"I'm definitely selling. I have an appraiser coming out to look over the property later today."

"I'll put my offer in the hat right now." He stated a price that made her toes curl. She stopped and stared. He must have taken her shock as disinterest, because before she could open her mouth to say anything, he upped his offer by half a million dollars. "We really want this house. Furnishings included. I don't want to play games with bidding wars or anything else. Name your price, and we'll settle the deal." He handed her another card. "No need to waste money on a real estate agent. I'm sure our attorneys can work the details out for us."

"As I said, I already have a real estate agent, and her appraisal is on the agenda. I have someone coming in to appraise the antiques, too. You're sure you want everything?"

"The wife says she wants the estate as is. She loved the way your mother-in-law decorated. Anything we don't like, we can unload later."

That said a lot about the woman's poor taste. Dark and dreary wasn't a trendy style. Not in Cameron's book anyway. "How soon would you want to move in?"

"As soon as it's available. We're willing to lease the property until the sale closes."

Cameron smiled. Eloise and Alfie would be free to come to Lullaby if that was the case. No headaches with auctions, open houses, etc. All loose ends would be tied up in one tidy little swoop. And the sweet lady from church that Cameron had called for the appraisal—a single mother with a newly absent ex-husband, a young baby that Cameron had recently delivered, and a stack of bills to pay—would walk away with a multi-million dollar deal that hadn't even caused her to break a sweat.

Thanks, Lord. Cameron smiled up at the sky, floored by the chain of events that were freeing her from the bonds that had caused her so much grief. One deal that would bless so many people. One deal that would put closure on all the loose ends in her life. "I'm sure we can work something out. I'll call you after the appraisal." She waved his card in the air.

His smile reminded her of the Cheshire cat. "I look forward to it."

She could feel his eyes on her as she continued her run. She completed her circuit—her final run through the area she'd never grown fond of—and hurried home to share the news.

"I sold the house and everything in it," she called out to whoever was within hearing range as soon as she'd cleared the front door.

Seth stepped around the corner of the sitting room. A clipboard rested on his arm, and his pen was poised over the paper. "I thought you were going on a run."

"I did." Cameron couldn't help but laugh at the confused expression on his face. "I went on a run and sold the house—lock, stock, and barrel."

"I'm not even sure what that means." Seth shook his head.

"I'm not either, but it suits my purpose." She laughed.

"The take away from the comment is, I sold *everything*. The house, the antiques—the buyer wants it all."

"I haven't even finished itemizing the antiques list. Did you agree on a price?"

"No. I haven't even committed the sale to him. I said the appraisers would be here soon, and I'd let him know after I talked to them."

"Your family had a lot of expensive things, Cam. I'm not sure an off-the-cuff offer would even begin to cover what the estate and antiques are worth. I'm glad you're having professionals come in. I'm writing out my best estimate on each item so you have something to go by, but you'll want to get the appraiser's opinion, too."

"I know what the last few homes have sold for in the area, and he offered a million more than the highest I've ever heard. For the antiques he added another half million."

He gulped. "Well, then, it looks like you'll have yourself a sale."

"That's what I'm thinking."

The doorbell rang, and Seth invited the antique appraiser inside.

"I need to run up and take a shower. Can you show him around, Seth?" She figured she could leave the job to him, since she had no clue what the items were worth.

He nodded, and she hurried up to her room. It was nice to have someone to lean on. She hurried through her shower and the routine of dressing, wanting to get to her grandfather's belongings. Eloise and Alfie had packed most of their belongings the night before. The day was moving along quickly, and if they hurried, they could leave by late afternoon for Lullaby.

Eloise met Cameron at her grandfather's door, her eyes huge. "You sold the house?"

"I did. How long do you think it'll take you and Alfie to finish packing your things?"

Her dear friend looked like she'd seen a ghost. "I don't suppose it'll take long at all. We only have the two small rooms. The furnishings aren't ours. We've learned to live light. Al has his tools down at the shed. He'd want to take those along. Other than that, we don't have much left to pack."

"Why don't you see if Al thinks it'll all fit in the estate's pickup truck? If it won't, we'll call for a moving van." She pulled a stack of shirts from her grandfather's drawer and set them aside.

Eloise hadn't moved.

"El, are you okay?"

"It's all going so fast."

Cameron stood and walked over to her. "I thought you'd be as ready to leave this place as I am. I didn't mean to rush you. If you want to stay longer, we'll arrange a later date for the sale. There's no need to hurry, not on your end. I'll wait to sell as long as you need me to."

"Oh, no you don't." Eloise rallied. "You aren't taking off and leavin' us behind again. I'm more than ready to get out of this place. I just didn't think it would go this fast. I thought you'd leave us behind and forget to come back for us."

Cam wrapped her arms around Eloise's soft body. "I wouldn't forget you. Not in a million years. But I'd rather take you along now. I'd rather not have a reason to ever see this place again."

"Works for me. I'd better round up that man of mine

and put him to work." She turned around. "The truck, you say?"

"Yes. Alfie's the only one who's ever driven it. He might as well keep it."

"Cammie, that shiny new truck is less than a year old! You can't just be givin' things away like that. You'll end up broke."

"I'm far from broke." Cameron smiled at El's use of her pet name. She walked back over to the dresser. "Alfie loves that truck, and you'll need wheels in Lullaby. It's so pretty there, Alfie will need something to drive you around in as you explore. You know, while you go on romantic Sunday afternoon drives or when you steal away for a private picnic in the hills?"

"Oh you."

Cameron could swear Eloise blushed.

"It's never too late for a second honeymoon, ya know. As a matter of fact, you two should spend some time seeing the world while you're at it." Cameron made a mental note to send them to some exotic places. They could consider it their retirement package. After all, what was the use of having money if you couldn't enjoy spending it on others?

"I know someone else who could benefit from a second honeymoon. A real one this time. With a real man like Seth."

"Eloise!" Cameron hissed. "What if Seth hears you?"

"Somebody call my name?" Seth peeked his head around the corner.

Cameron flushed with embarrassment. "Nope."

The appraiser followed Seth into the room.

Eloise clamped her lips together to hide her smile and started emptying Cameron's grandfather's top drawers while Cameron focused on the lower ones.

The jeans and slacks were easy. She slipped them into the box. But his shirts were another story. While her grandfather hadn't been an affectionate man, he had learned to be there for her during the final year of her marriage. He'd stood up to Jim when Jim's posture became menacing or his words turned to threats. He'd held her when Jim had pushed her to tears. His flannel shirts represented a security she hadn't had until that point.

Cameron held up a worn, blue-and-green plaid flannel shirt and smiled. It was one of her grandfather's favorites, and by association hers, too. "I loved this shirt. How am I going to let these things go?"

The men were muttering at the far side of the room.

Eloise placed a stack of white T-shirts into the box. "I say you don't. Pack them in a separate box and take them home with you. You'll know what to do with them when the time comes."

"That's a wonderful idea. Thanks, El."

Seth and the appraiser moved on to another room.

Cameron went through every pocket of every item as she packed her grandfather's belongings. He had been a simple man, not one to put much value on things. They'd lived a minimalist life together, and that hadn't changed when Cameron begged him to move in with her at the estate.

They carried his suits down to the garage and placed them with the other donation items. The truck would stop by for pickup later that afternoon.

Once back upstairs, Cameron surveyed the room, her grandfather's life reduced to a few brown cardboard boxes. The special box of shirts had been carried to her bedroom so it didn't get mixed up with the donations. "I guess that's it."

"I guess so." Eloise reached for a box.

"No ma'am. I don't want you carrying that heavy box downstairs. You'd better head out and finish packing your own things."

"If you're sure." Eloise left the room with the extra brown packing boxes in her arms.

Cameron lifted a box to carry downstairs.

Seth met her in the hall. "The appraisal is finished. Here, you take the paperwork. I'll carry the box."

Cameron sent Seth a look he couldn't read and made the switch.

Seth raised his eyebrows in surprise. "What, no argument?"

"I'm drained. I don't know if it was the run this morning or the packing, or maybe just the mental exhaustion from all the plans and thinking, but I'm whopped."

She did look unusually tired. Dark circles carved out crescents under her blue eyes. Her usually perfect ponytail had slipped to the side.

"Why don't you sit down over there and look over the numbers? I was purposefully low on every item, but the neighbor's bid easily covers the worth of the antiques. Pending the numbers on the house appraisal, I'd say you have a done deal."

Cameron carried the clipboard toward the wing chair, her gait dragging, and settled onto it. She curled her legs up under her and leaned her head against the back. "You take that box down, and I'll grab one to carry when you come back. Maybe if I just sit here a moment I'll get a second wind."

Seth did as she asked, but he was worried. He'd never seen the bouncy side of Cameron give way to exhaustion. Maybe she'd caught a bug. He decided to hunt down Eloise for a second opinion.

He found her in her suite. "I'm worried about Cam. Did she seem off to you this morning?"

"Not at all. She's on cloud nine with everything going so smoothly. She's probably a bit drained from going through her grandfather's things. That can wear even the most perky person down."

"I think it's more than that. Can you come back up and see if she's running a fever or something? I think she'll be more open to a mother's touch in this kind of situation."

"Mm-hmm." She surveyed him.

"I'm not the one needing an appraisal, El." Seth fidgeted under her scrutiny.

"Oh, you're needin' somethin', all right. You're needin' a woman's opinion and comin' 'round here askin' me when you could just as easily find a woman of your own to ask. Cameron would happily give you her opinions to all your questions and comments if you took the time to ask her."

"I'm sure she would, but I just want to make sure she's all right, and I know she won't be receptive to my fussing over her."

"You afraid of that girl, Seth?"

"A little. She doesn't like it when I fuss over her."

"You fuss over her often?" A huge smile lit Eloise's face.

"No. I don't think I fuss over her at all, but she sure takes it that way."

"I see."

Perplexed, Seth stared at her. "*What* do you see?"

"Two crazy stubborn people who don't want to acknowledge what's right in front of their faces—that's what I see."

More confused than ever, Seth decided to let it go. "So is that a yes? Will you come and check on her?"

Eloise stomped out of the room ahead of him, muttering under her breath about love and mulish people and something about having to go all the way to Lullaby to set things straight.

Cameron slept soundly in the chair, the clipboard still clutched in her hand.

Eloise stopped short. "Well, I'll be."

"I told you something's up with her." Seth crossed his arms and tried not to look too smug.

"Even during the worst times I ain't never seen her fall asleep sittin' up like this." She looked back at Seth. "And I've seen this girl go through some *hard* times."

Seth sobered. They walked over to Cam's chair.

Eloise reached out to feel her forehead. "No fever."

"What do we do now?"

"We let the girl sleep. She's likely exhausted. She never sleeps as well as she thinks she does in this house, and the storm last night didn't help matters." She grabbed a blanket from the end of Cameron's grandfather's bed and draped it over her. She gently moved the clipboard to the bed.

"*If* you can work quietly, you can carry the other boxes down to the garage. After that, if you want somethin' else to do, you can go out to the shed and help Al pack his tools."

"I'd love to help." Seth stacked two boxes and headed for the stairs. He wondered about Eloise's statement as they made their way to the first level. Cam seemed to have a great affection for her grandfather, but she also seemed to hate the house they'd lived in. "Eloise, why does Cam hate this house so much?"

"I think I'd better leave that for her to tell. She'll tell you when she's good and ready. As I said upstairs, she's had some hard times here."

The ringtone on Seth's phone played the theme song of the old cartoon, *Josie and the Pussycats*. He set the boxes down with the others in the garage and frowned. He'd chosen specific ringtones for each of his friends. Why would Josie be calling him? It probably had something to do with the eviction. "Hey Josie, Seth here. How's it going?"

"Not so great. I hate to be calling you like this, but there's been an accident. Your Aunt Ginny fell down the stairs and broke her leg. Are you still in Kansas City?"

Seth straightened, suddenly alert. "I am. Aunt Ginny broke her leg? How on earth did she manage that?"

"All I know is that she fell down the stairs. I was at the Landing, packing, so I don't have all the details. Mandy's at the hospital with her, and she's promised to call as soon as she knows more about what's going on. I hurried back to cover at the inn, which is where I am right now."

Seth sat on one of the boxes. "How'd you find out? Who found her?" Seth felt awful that this happened to Aunt Ginny when he'd left her alone. "Did she lie there in pain all night?"

"No, it happened this morning."

Seth slumped in relief.

"I'd met one of the guests at the inn yesterday while I was there getting my baked goods, and I gave her my card so she could stop by Caleb's candy shop during my shift. The guest found your aunt this morning and called an ambulance then called me since she didn't know anyone else. I sent Mandy right over to the hospital."

"I'm glad the woman called you. Remind me to comp her stay. I'll finish up here and head straight home." He exhaled and stood.

"Wait. Slow down. Ginny told us about the inspection, and Mandy and I were already planning to move in later today. I'll cover for you at the inn until you get here. We're off through Monday, so don't break your neck getting home. Mandy and I can cover things until you get back."

He opened the door to the house and paused. "I appreciate it, Josie. We only have a couple of regulars staying there for now. Can you handle a light lunch and put something on for dinner? You know the types of things Aunt Ginny fixed. I'm sure she has the pantry and refrigerator full of items to choose from. She usually has a few backup items in the freezer, too. Check there first. If you need to, have something delivered from town."

"We'll be fine. You just focus on getting Cam's loose ends tied up, and we'll take care of everything until you get here."

He walked inside and shut the door behind him. "You're a lifesaver, Josie. Caleb got a good one when he found you."

"There are a few other good ones around, ya know, if you open your eyes to see them."

"You, too?" He slumped against the door. "Everyone has to get in on the matchmaking scene. It's an epidemic."

"What?" Josie's voice was all innocence. "I was just making a statement."

Seth chose to ignore the topic. "I'm going to let you go so I can call the hospital."

"Call if it makes you feel better, but Ginny's sedated for now. She's in good hands. We'll let you know if anything changes."

Chapter 7

"Hey Ginny! How are you feeling?" Cameron slid through the partially opened hospital door and entered the dimly lit patient room.

"Cameron! What a nice surprise." Ginny shifted on the bed.

Cameron hurried over to help Ginny sit higher against the pillows. Her injured leg was encased in a large cast.

"And since you asked, what I'm feeling is agitated, impatient, and frustrated. I can't get out of this bed to do anything, and I've been cooped up for the better part of a week. This place is driving me crazy."

"That's why we came. Seth and I are ready to break you out of here." Cameron reached over and turned on the bedside lamp. "At this very moment, your doctor is at the nurse's station filling out your release papers.

Seth's signing off on them. I thought I'd sneak in and give you a heads-up."

"Really?" Ginny's eyes brightened. "I get to go home today?"

"Right now." Cameron pushed the controls to make the bed sit up and then lowered it. "Let's get you dressed and ready before the men get here."

"Oh, goodness." Ginny reached up to fluff her hair. "I don't think I have enough time."

"You look fine. All we're going to do is move you home to your suite. We'll get you presentable so you look good while we go through the hospital, but no one's going to see you otherwise." She handed Ginny her makeup kit. "You fool around with that while I get your clothes out of this bag that I brought along."

Cameron helped Ginny into a pretty sweatshirt and matching pair of loose sweatpants. They were ready and waiting a few minutes later when Seth entered the room with a wheelchair.

The doctor followed on Seth's heels. "I understand you're ready to go home."

"Beyond ready. I can't believe a little infection caused me to sit here for a week."

"Those little infections can be nasty. Trust me, it's better to deal with one here than after you return home. Now you can concentrate on getting up and around without worrying about anything else."

"That's good to know."

"I have information in this packet that you'll need as you adjust." He held up a folder with his medical practice's logo on it. "I want you to get settled in before you worry about getting up and around. Once you're comfortable and feel up to it, you need to start physical therapy." He glanced over his glasses to make sure

Ginny was listening. "Since today is Friday, I'd like to see you in physical therapy by Monday. They'll get you set up and help you figure out how to get around safely. You'll have someone staying with you at all times?"

Cameron spoke up. "I'll be with her."

"You'll be in good hands with Cameron. Seth, you'll be handy, too?"

"I'll be there, yes. I can help her get around or help her do whatever she needs to do."

"In that case, I'll see you in my office soon for a follow-up. The information is in the packet. Call if you need anything."

"I will, Doc." Ginny was already sliding from the bed.

Seth and Cameron hurried over to offer their support. They eased her into the wheelchair and gathered up her belongings.

Seth stood with hands on hips, surveying the vegetation that filled the room. "I'm going to need a separate trip to gather all the flowers. And we already brought home all those armloads each day."

"Your room at the inn looks like a flower shop." Cameron agreed.

Ginny nodded toward some potted tulips. "Give me that newest plant, the one on my bedside, and I'll have the nurse donate the rest of them to other patients who don't have anything in their rooms."

"What a sweet idea, Ginny!" Cameron started plucking the notes and cards from the arrangements. "You'll want these for thank-you cards."

Seth didn't waste any time darting out the door to tell the nurse. He returned, plopped the coveted plant on Ginny's lap and wheeled the chair toward the door.

"In a hurry, Seth?" Cameron's voice dripped with amused sarcasm.

"I don't really like hospitals."

Ginny snickered. "He spent enough time in them as a boy. I'm sure he doesn't."

"Accident prone, hmm?" Cameron laughed.

"A total daredevil." Ginny chuckled. "I don't think I can remember a time when the boy wasn't in a cast, a coma, or that he didn't have stitches on one body part or another."

"That's terrible."

"It certainly made for a stressful life. If we'd had speed dial back then, emergency would have been number one on the list."

Seth didn't comment. He continued at a fast clip, headed for the elevator.

"We aren't rushing her to surgery, you know," Cameron called to his retreating back.

"I want out of this place. The smells, the way the sounds echo with all the linoleum and metal." He shuddered. "I don't see how you can work here day in and day out."

"I don't mind, but I mostly work outside the hospital setting." Cameron was nearly running to keep up. "Being out of the hospital and delivering babies in a warmer, more natural setting is the reason I picked a career as a nurse-midwife. Well, that and the fact that I love babies and deliveries and everything about pregnancy."

"You're weird." Seth glanced back at her with a flippant grin.

"Seth! Cameron is *not* weird," Ginny said. "Apologize at once."

"You're talking to me like I'm eight." Seth side-stepped her command and poked at the down-arrow button.

"You sound like you're eight."

Seth radiated nervous energy.

Ginny rolled her eyes. "And stand still. You don't have to tap your foot with impatience just because the elevator isn't here yet. It'll come when it comes."

Seth grinned at Cameron, and her heart fluttered. Her stomach was certainly doing weird things, especially when he was around. But she wasn't about to admit that to him.

"Shouldn't it be here by now?" Seth reached over and pushed the down button three more times.

"Pushing the button doesn't make the elevator car come any faster." Cameron stated the obvious.

"Really?" Seth pushed the button with purpose three more times while staring her down. "I would never have known."

"Sarcasm now. Is that really necessary?"

"Apparently." Ginny laced a finger in the belt loop of Seth's jeans and tugged him away from the button. "Just pray the car comes before he heads for the stairs."

The doors opened at that moment, and Seth expertly wheeled Ginny in. For all his obnoxious energy and eagerness to leave the hospital behind, he was as gentle as ever with Ginny's care.

"Ground floor, here we come." His foot was tapping again.

Ginny grasped Cameron's hand. "How are Eloise and Al settling in?"

"They're doing fine. They're thriving, actually. Eloise loved meeting you and said she wants to do you proud in the kitchen. She's been cooking up a storm ever since."

"She's great." Seth agreed. "And Alfie jumped right in to help with the renovations. He's gifted at construction."

"He's gifted at gardening, too. Wait until you see what he does with the grounds."

"I saw what he did with your estate. He does great work. I'm more than happy to let him putter around."

"They want to feel they're earning their keep since you won't let them pay for their suite. Eloise said she's never seen anything like it."

Seth laughed. "After living at the estate? That place was gorgeous."

"Did you not notice how dark and austere that place was? Eloise hated it as much as I did. We were both happy when our neighbor agreed to our final asking price. As soon as we close on the house, that part of our life will be behind us." Cameron saw the confusion that clouded Seth's features. She didn't want to answer his questions. Not yet anyway. "Oh look, ground floor! Seth, why don't you go and get the car, and I'll wheel Ginny outside when you get here."

The elevator door opened, and Seth guided Ginny out. He parked her wheelchair in an alcove at the left of the double doors.

"I'll meet you out front." He held his hand out for Cameron's keys.

Ginny watched with interest as Cameron dug through her purse.

Cameron didn't miss the way her eyes took in the interaction. "We figured it'd be easier for you to slip into my car than it would be to climb up into Seth's truck."

"Oh, heavens. Good choice. I can't even imagine trying to get up into the cab of that thing."

"Now my truck's a thing? I thought you liked it."

"I love it, hon." She patted his arm. "Now go get my chariot. This princess wants to get home."

Cameron handed him the keys, and he jogged out the doors. "Couldn't get out of here fast enough, could he?" The fast pace of his escape made her laugh. "He really doesn't like hospitals, does he?"

"Hates them with a passion. Did you notice how often he visited me this week? Twice. Once when I first came in, so he could convince himself that I was really okay. Once when he couldn't find anyone else to bring me my slippers."

"I would have brought them! I didn't know he had such a hospital phobia."

"You were at the clinic. I needed them right then."

"Oh. That makes sense."

"It didn't help that his parents were in the hospital for weeks before he lost them. He was six, and they'd been in a bad car accident. That's when he came to live with me."

"I didn't know." She guessed she could count her blessings that her parents' passing was swift. She hadn't had time to say good-bye, let alone have to watch them live in pain at a hospital.

"Of course you didn't know." Ginny patted her hand. "But that's why he truly hates hospitals. I have to say you, Josie, Mandy, and Eloise have been wonderful about helping out and standing in the gap for me. And I've grown very fond of Eloise after our evening chats and card games at my hospital bed. I see why you love her so much."

Cameron's heart melted. "I'm so glad to hear that. I want Eloise to fit in and find her place here."

"She has a place, as far as I'm concerned." Ginny looked at Cameron with sharp eyes. "So now that Seth's gone, what's the story with the estate? I can't imagine you'd hate your grandfather's place that much. From what I've seen, you loved him too much for that."

"It's complicated." Cameron hedged.

"I can handle complicated. Trust me to listen, Cameron. You've been here for me. Let me be there for you."

Cameron squatted down in front of her friend. She rested her arms on her legs, clasped her hands, and looked out the front doors to make sure Seth was really gone.

He hadn't yet reached her car. Now that he had cleared the hospital doors, he walked slowly, leisurely. He held her key chain in his hand and rubbed it with his thumb. She willed him to walk faster.

Ginny reached out and clutched Cameron's hands. "Tell me, dear."

Cameron sighed. "The estate belonged to my deceased husband and his mother. His name was Jim. He passed away in June."

"Oh honey. I'm so sorry." Compassion shone from her eyes. "Now it's my turn to say I had no idea."

"No. Wait, please. I didn't tell anyone besides Josie. I wanted it that way." Cameron tried to choose her words carefully, but there weren't very many ways to say what Ginny needed to know. She swallowed. "My marriage wasn't a happy one. My mother-in-law hated me and everything I did. She never wanted her son to marry, and she sure didn't want him to marry me, so I became an instant enemy when we said our vows. I thought Jim had wanted a private wedding because he was in such a hurry to marry me—and he was, but not because he was head over heels like I thought. He wanted to avoid a prewedding confrontation with his mother. He used me to prove a point—that she couldn't control him anymore."

Ginny listened, Cameron's hand still clutched in both of hers. Her eyes reflected her sorrow. "He wasn't head over heels in love with you?"

"No. He just wanted to show his mother he could make his own choices, that she didn't fully control him. That was it."

"So she controlled him to a point?"

"Their relationship was very dysfunctional. But she hated me and made it clear with every breath she took. And I hated every second we lived in that house."

"Your husband didn't intervene?"

"He worked every moment he possibly could. He was an obstetrician, and he also taught college classes and stayed late every night."

"You deserved better." Ginny's sweet affection brought tears to Cameron's eyes. She blinked them back.

"Anyway"—Cameron took a deep breath and blew it out slowly—"she passed away two years ago, and I thought maybe things would improve. Instead, they got worse. He started drinking heavily, and he became violent."

Ginny's eyes narrowed. "He didn't hurt you…"

"No. He never laid a hand on me. He threw things, became erratic, but it was scary all the same. I never knew when he'd decide to turn the anger toward me." She hesitated. "I was relieved just over a year ago when he decided to leave me. We were separated until June, then he asked for one more chance. We tried to reconcile but realized it was a mistake pretty much from the start." She glanced at the door again, but Seth still hadn't returned with her car. She spoke quickly to get the words out. "So Jim said he'd file divorce papers. I never received mine, so I called last month and found out he'd hit a tree later that day, driving drunk. He never made it to the attorney's office."

"Oh, my goodness." Ginny raised a hand to her mouth. "What a horrible thing to find out. You should have told us. We all would have been there for you. You must know that."

Cameron gripped Ginny's warm hand. "But this is exactly why I didn't tell you. I don't want my past to mess up my future. I never intended to have a failed marriage." She took a deep breath. "I don't exactly want to broadcast the fact to everyone in Lullaby. I just want a fresh start."

"You didn't fail anything, Cam. Your husband and his mother failed you." A knowing smile softened Ginny's lips. "Your story explains so much. You never put on airs. You care so much about others. But there's been a heaviness underneath that I've never understood. You need to let go of those burdens, lay them at the cross. You want a fresh start? Let go of everything you left behind and embrace the newness of now."

"I'm not holding on," Cameron said. "I don't think I am, anyway."

"You said yourself you never planned to divorce. You're holding on to that. Did you try your best? Did you want to make your marriage work?"

"Of course I did. Eloise can attest to how hard I tried." The tears pooled and threatened to overflow.

"Eloise doesn't need to tell me anything. I already know you. You wear your heart on your sleeve. You're the type to go over and beyond in a relationship, even when the odds are stacked against you." She placed her other hand on top of Cameron's. "Let go, Cameron, and move on. I want to see the sadness disappear from your eyes. No more looking back, no more holding back. See what God has for you. Let Him restore your joy. Why do you think He brought you to Lullaby?"

Cameron thought about that for a moment. "He wanted me to find peace, to have a fresh start."

"Does that make you feel guilty?"

She frowned. "I feel guilty that I'm so relieved to be here. How can that be? If I'm supposed to be here, why can't I have peace?"

"What I think is, deep down, you knew you'd tried as hard as a person can try. It was time to cut your losses and move on. Jim offered you another chance, and you gave it to him. It didn't work. Your husband was an idiot not to see the gift he got when he married you."

"Oh Ginny." Cameron couldn't help but laugh through her tears. "Thank you."

Seth swung the car onto the curved lane in front of the hospital and pulled up to the automatic door.

Cameron stood and wiped the few wayward tears that had found their way down her cheeks.

Ginny glanced outside then turned back to her. "I mean it. I've seen your beauty in action. Not just outward beauty, but inward beauty. My nephew is a tough nut to crack, and even he can see the good in you. You're turning his head in a way no one else has ever managed to do. He's had his share of pain. He's grown into a loving man, but he chooses to hold everyone at arm's length. You have the ability to break through that facade. I think God sent you here for some very specific purposes. I think you and my nephew will find happiness through the adventure. But for now, I'll keep my lips sealed."

Seth opened the front door of the car and slid his

frame from the front seat with a grace most men couldn't manage if they tried. He saw them watching him and grinned. He rounded the car, heading for the doors.

"Let's give him some grace and meet him outside," Cameron suggested. "He looks so happy, I'd hate to see that great mood disappear by making him come back inside."

She waved him away. He grinned with relief and headed back to the car.

"See what I mean? You have a huge heart. One last question—who watched out for you at the estate? Who kept you sane while living inside that dark place?"

"God was in that dark place with me. And Eloise and Alfie kept me sane. They went to bat for me when Jim started berating me."

"No wonder you adore them so much."

" 'Tis true. If they weren't there, Jim might have been more violent. I don't know."

"Eloise adores you."

"I adore her, too." Cam bent down to give Ginny a quick hug. "And now I have you and Seth and Josie and Caleb and Brit and Matt, amongst others."

"Thanks for bringing me into the circle by trusting me with your story. Better late than never."

Seth was moving things around on the backseat.

Cameron laughed. "You've always been in my circle, Ginny. You took me in the moment you knew I'd taken the job as nurse-midwife. I don't know how I'd have adjusted if you hadn't been there for me. It was a culture shock to come from Kansas City to this small town. You filled in the gap when I had to leave Al and Eloise behind. I missed them terribly."

"Well, they're here for you now."

She wheeled Ginny out the front doors and over to the car.

Seth stood beside the car holding the back door open. "It's about time. I thought you two were going to stand in there talking all afternoon."

"We had things that needed to be discussed."

"What kinds of things? Couldn't they have waited until we got home? I thought for a minute I was going to have to go back in after you." He shuddered. "Let's get you out of here."

"So dramatic," Ginny muttered. She put her hands on the armrests and attempted to stand.

"No, wait!" Seth hurried to his aunt's side.

Cameron studied the situation, trying to figure out the best way to get Ginny out of the chair and into the car without hitting the cast or hurting her leg.

Before she came up with a plan, Seth had swung Ginny up into his arms. "Change of plans. Move the wheelchair and open the front passenger door. I don't think we'll be able to get her in the backseat with this cast. If you put the front seat all the way back, I think we'll make it work with her up front."

Cameron did as he asked. She slipped the overnight bag onto the floor to prop up Ginny's leg and watched as Seth gently eased her into the passenger seat.

It was far easier to maneuver Ginny into her suite at the inn. Seth carried her up the front porch stairs and placed her into the wheelchair waiting just inside the front door. He wheeled her back toward her rooms that opened off the kitchen.

Eloise met them in the kitchen and busied herself with fussing over Ginny. "I have everythin' ready for you in your room. You don't worry about anything, ya hear? Dinner is in the oven, and all the sides are prepped. I can sit with you for a while before we need to serve. I don't care whether you want to sleep or if you want to talk, I'm here for you." She turned to Cameron. "You run along now. I know you had one more appointment later this afternoon."

"I have time, El." Cameron laughed. She'd had no idea Eloise and Ginny would hit it off so well, but she was thrilled to see the bond begin to form. Both women deserved to slow down and take more time for themselves. They could share some of the work load and have fun in the process.

"Where did that nephew of mine situate everyone?" Ginny asked Eloise as they disappeared from the kitchen.

"Seth moved out of his suite and into the carriage house out back so that Al and I could move into his suite across the hall from the kitchen. That allowed me to be close to the kitchen and close to you. Cameron moved her things into your extra room so she'll be close by if you need her durin' the night. You're going to need help to the bathroom and such. I'm here for you, too. And Seth said to call him anytime he's needed. Whatever you need, don't you hesitate to ask."

"Looks like they have everything under control," Cameron said. She glanced over at Seth.

He was staring at the empty doorway where they'd disappeared. "Yep. Looks like it." He turned to her. "I appreciate all the help and the use of your car."

"It was nothing." She smiled.

He reached up and twirled a strand of her hair. "It wasn't 'nothing.' It was sweet. Aunt Ginny loves having you around. You made the transition from hospital to home easier."

She wondered if he loved having her around.

"I owe you."

"After everything you've done for me? And for Eloise and Alfie? You don't owe me a thing."

"Yes I do. I owe you, and I won't take no for an answer. I want to take you to dinner." His dimples flashed. "Will you stop arguing and let me treat you to a special night out?"

Who was she to turn down a dinner invite from a grateful friend? Especially one with dimples as cute as his. "I'd love to have dinner with you."

Chapter 8

It's just a date between friends.

Cameron growled in frustration as she tossed another pair of slacks onto the growing pile of clothes that lay on her bed. She reached into the closet for her last pair of pants. How could she have outgrown every item she owned overnight? It wasn't like people had growth spurts at this point in life.

She surveyed the wreckage and wondered if she wasn't being a tad bit picky. She was going out with Seth, after all. She liked him a lot and wanted to make a good impression. But at the same time, she hadn't dated in years and wasn't sure now was a good time to start.

The thought was punctuated by the ever-present queasiness that rolled over her. She took a few deep breaths to ward it off. It would be fine. She would be fine. She liked Seth. He liked her. They were *friends*.

So if he was more friend than date—the outing was no big deal.

Therefore, the clothing issue had nothing to do with the newness of the dating situation. It had nothing to do with Seth. He always made her feel comfortable in his presence. If it wasn't a case of not finding the right outfit for the "date," then what was it?

Her nerves frayed some more.

"Okay, Cameron. Let's go through this one more time." She looked forward to the outing, she couldn't wait to spend some time alone in Seth's company. The only times she'd seen him over the past couple of weeks, they'd either been at meals with multiple people present, they'd been helping with the youth, or they'd been helping Ginny or Eloise with one thing or another. Until today. She wasn't nervous about the date. She wasn't being picky about her outfits, finding fault out of nerves.

She slipped into her last pair of black pants. No deal. They wouldn't button. This was ridiculous! None of the slacks fit quite right. They all had waist issues. Why hadn't she noticed this before? She thought for a moment. She always wore scrubs or yoga pants at work under her lab jacket. She liked to be comfortable, and with births taking their sweet time for the most part, the job required a lot of sitting around and waiting. When she came home she crawled into her comfort clothes and settled in for the night.

Ever since Ginny's accident, she and Ginny had taken to eating dinner in their suite while watching old movies. It was easier for Ginny to eat from a tray at the sitting-room couch than to sit at the table with guests. They never could figure out how to prop her leg up in a way that would allow her to be comfortable without taking up chair space. Cameron didn't want her friend eating alone, so she joined her. Besides, after a day of talking to patients and coworkers, Cameron preferred the intimacy of a quiet dinner in their suite.

The only downside to the situation was lost time in Seth's company. They all felt it best if at least one person from the inn dined with the guests, and Eloise was too busy managing the food to sit and visit.

Eloise. It was her fault Cameron's pants didn't fit! Cameron smiled. Eloise had been at the inn for three weeks, and Cameron couldn't seem to say no to seconds of all her wonderful down-home cooking these days—even with the nervous stomach that had plagued her since the news of Jim's passing. It was ridiculous! The woman was doing her job as substitute chef just a little bit too well.

She'd figure out how to avoid the second helpings later, but for now, Cameron had a dinner date in less than twenty minutes and couldn't for the life of her figure out an outfit that would work. A dress would be too...well, dressy, and most of her dresses had fitted waists. Nerves continued to toy with her stomach. *Just a thank-you dinner between friends, Cam, chill out!* Cameron closed her eyes, took a deep breath, and slowly blew out. Ten minutes until he came for her. She needed to focus.

He'd said to dress casual. She glanced up at the shelf that held her yoga pants. They were casual. But more importantly, they were stretchy. Yoga pants also screamed, "I'm not over-dressing for you, this is just a casual date between friends." Not even a date really, more like a celebratory meal to recognize that the craziness of the past few weeks was behind them, and life could now settle down into a predictable rhythm. At least, in Cameron's eyes that's all the date represented. Or so she told herself. Futilely. Her stomach roiled.

Why had she said yes?

A knock at the door made her jump.

"I'm not ready."

"It's me, Cammie. Let me in." Eloise's no-nonsense voice carried through the door.

Cameron turned the knob.

"Your date is in less than five minutes and you haven't shown your face. What's goin' on in here? You gettin' a last minute case of nerves? 'Cause if you are, you don't need to with that man. He's nothing but sweet yumminess on a platter, and you need to just go out with him and have a good time."

Sweet yumminess on a platter? Nope, no pressure there.

Only after her spiel did Eloise notice that Cameron stood before her in her underclothes.

"You ain't even dressed yet? Girl, what's the matter with you? You can't keep that man waitin'!"

"I can't find anything that fits."

"What do you mean, you can't find anythin'? I've seen your pile of clothes. Move aside and let me take a look."

There wasn't much for Eloise to look at, since her entire collection of clothing lay in a heap on the bed.

"I didn't bring everything with me when I came here. I left behind a lot of, shall we say, baggage."

"You can say that again." Eloise pursed her lips and surveyed the pile of clothes. "What's wrong with these?" She held up the black slacks. "Dressy casual."

"None of my clothes fit."

"Take these slacks and slip them on. Maybe I can rig the button real quick. Why won't they fit?"

Cameron shrugged, not willing to share her theory. She did as she was told.

Eloise tugged at the button and loop but didn't have any better luck than Cameron did. "There's nothin' I can do to fix this. At least not in the time we have allotted." She frowned at Cameron's stomach. "You're still slender as ever, but you been eatin' up a storm lately. You ain't gonna be forced into these slacks any day soon, not today anyway."

It was her opening. "I blame your good cooking."

Eloise gave her *the look*. "It wasn't my cookin' that put you in this situation. Your lack of willpower ain't my responsibility. I might cook a good meal, but it's the eater who has the responsibility to just say no. And apparently, you ain't been sayin' no often enough."

Seth's voice carried through the wooden door. "Uh, Cam? It's me, Seth. Ginny told me to knock. Eloise isn't around or I'd have, um, had her call for you. I just wanted to let you know I'm here. I'll wait in the sitting room with Aunt Ginny. No hurry."

"Thanks, Seth. I'll be right there." He sounded as nervous as the men who were unwittingly dragged into the clinic. Cameron reached for the yoga pants. She lowered her voice and hissed at Eloise, "He's here, and I'm not ready!"

"You will be." Eloise glanced at the black leggings and reached for a long blue, purple, and black baby-doll style shirt that tied in the back. "This'll look cute and trendy with the tight leggin's. It's fitted, but not too fitted. Wear those black slip-on shoes and you'll be fine."

Cameron slipped the shirt over her head and tied it. "Thanks, Eloise. You're a lifesaver."

* * *

"I never figured you for the Thai food kind of person." Cameron faced the table. Two steps led up to the private booth, the third step being the bench itself that wrapped around all four sides of the table. The table seemed to set down into the floor, but really it was the illusion of the steps that gave the impression. Cameron slipped her shoes off and slid across the cushion of the wooden bench. Tall walls on either end of each booth made their table feel intimate. A large mirror filled the back wall, adding a sense of spaciousness to the cozy area.

"Are you kidding?" Seth slid in beside her. "I love Thai food. That's what you get for trying to prejudge me, trying to put me in a box."

"I'm not trying to judge you." Cameron laughed. "I just figured you for more of a meat-and-potatoes kind of guy."

"Figured, huh? You've been trying to figure me out?"

"I didn't say that."

"Yes, you pretty much did."

It was the perfect time for a change of subject. "This is a really nice place."

Seth grinned, making it clear he'd noticed the not-so-clever avoidance of his question. He reached for his cloth-napkin-wrapped silverware. "I'm glad you like it. Nothing's too good when it comes to a meal between friends, right?"

Cameron wondered if he was trying to lighten the mood or reinforce the friendship angle. Maybe he felt as nervous as she did. She glanced up at him. He didn't look nervous. He looked as comfortable—and as handsome—as ever.

Her mouth went dry. "A meal between friends. Right."

Whatever his intent, the point was made, the line was drawn, and she'd do her part to stick to the parameters. The thought actually calmed her. He'd reinforced what she'd been telling herself all day.

"I've never actually been here before," Seth admitted. "The restaurant hasn't been here all that long, and one of the guests at the inn told me about it the other night at dinner. It sounded perfect for our date."

Now he'd said *date*. Cameron was confused. So was it a date? Or was it a meal between friends? Or was it a friend date? And was there such a thing?

Her expression must have shown her confusion. When she didn't answer, he looked dismayed. "Do you even like Thai food? I didn't think to ask. We can leave and go somewhere else..."

"No, I love Thai. This is fine." She glanced at her shoes near the steps and smiled.

"What's so funny?" Seth's eyebrow quirked up, and his left dimple showed. "I'm serious. We can make a run for it if you want to."

"I don't want to. I was just picturing us trying to make a quick getaway out of here."

He smiled. "Yeah. I guess it would be sort of awkward." He set his silverware aside and placed his napkin on his lap.

Cameron had scooted in and settled at the inside wall of the table, her back to the mirror, while Seth had settled on the bench to her right. The arrangement felt cozy, intimate. Soft music played in the background, white linen covered the table, and a candle arrangement sat in the center. The glow played across Seth's features, softening them. Cameron could only hope the atmosphere was as friendly to her appearance. What if the candlelight washed her out? Made her look as sickly as she felt.

"You look beautiful tonight. Radiant. Getting out suits you."

There he went again, reading her mind.

"The company suits me." She felt herself blush. She couldn't believe she just said that. "And the surroundings. Yes. It's pretty here. Nice. I like it. You made a good choice." She rued her nervous rambling tongue.

"I'm glad you think so."

The waiter brought glasses of water filled with ice.

"No lemon, please." Cam covered the rim as the waiter tried to place a slice on her glass.

"None for me either." Seth echoed. He waited until the waiter walked off. "You must watch the same late-night talk shows as I do—the ones that show how dirty the lemons can be?"

"Ew, exactly."

"Makes you hesitant to eat out at all sometimes, ya know?"

"I do. Trust me, I learned enough in my microbiology classes to make a person never want to leave their house."

"But yet you leave anyway."

"That's because I had a great professor who taught us that germs are everywhere, and if we become too phobic, we won't have a life. Exposure to germs helps us build resistance. So it's all good. To a point." She laughed. "I still don't like dirty lemons stuck on top of my drink glasses."

"I hear you."

An awkward silence filled the air.

Seth squirmed. "Look, I'm not sure you can tell,

but I'm new to this dating thing. I know I'm pushing the friend angle pretty hard, but the truth is, I haven't dated since my broken engagement—"

"You were *engaged*?" Cameron stage whispered, leaning forward. She didn't know why she lowered her voice—it wasn't like anyone could hear them from their cozy habitat—but the revelation seemed to require a certain level of decorum. "I didn't see that coming."

"Um, yeah. A few years back." He looked nervous. "Is that a problem?"

"No. Not at all. I mean, I'm just surprised. I didn't figure you for the commitment type."

"There's that 'figuring' thing again. Do you really find me that fascinating?"

"No. Yes. That's a trick question, isn't it?"

"It wasn't meant to be a trick question at all." His smile was back, the nervousness gone. "I just wanted to explain that I don't take this date lightly. I don't want to overplay the friend angle."

"Gotcha."

No pressure there! She twisted and untwisted the napkin in her lap.

"I'm trying to balance the friend angle and date angle by explaining, but maybe now I'm tilting the scale too far to the date angle over the friend angle?"

"No. I think you're doing fine. I understand completely." That was an understatement. But she didn't feel now was the time to go into her failed marriage and Jim's passing. She smoothed out the napkin and forced her hands to still. "Maybe we should let the scale fall somewhere in between and see how things go from there."

"So friends with the option to date?"

"Perfect."

"Works for me." He seemed relieved.

She smiled. "I like the way you just lay it all out there on the table."

"I don't see why people have to sidestep so many issues. Why not just say what you're thinking and move on? Communication is really important to a relationship."

"Says the man I'd pegged as the strong, silent type."

He laughed. "Why don't you stop trying to peg me and see what you come up with by spending time with the real thing?"

"I'm doing that now."

"So you are."

"And I'm a science major, remember? I study, and then I make my deductions. I've been watching you for a while." She felt the blush roll up her cheeks as soon as the words were out. "I mean, we went on that Branson trip with the youth in August, and we hung out. Not to mention all the times we've worked together with the youth group over the past couple of months. And don't forget, we spent the weekend together at the estate. It's only natural that I've noticed things about you."

"What kinds of things?"

"Huh?"

"What kind of things have you noticed?" He rested his cheek on his hand, staring at her intently. "What kind of character do I portray?"

"Oh, um…" She had his full attention, which made the nerves return. "You—well, like right now. You give the person talking your full attention."

"Good. That's something I'd want to be known for."

"You stand by your word. You're a man of action— you don't just spout off ideas, you jump in to see them to fruition."

"Thank you for noticing." His dimple flashed as he settled against the back of the booth. "Anything else?"

"You're a man of integrity. You don't need to be at the forefront of things in order to do a good job. You work hard, no matter what job position you're in."

"You have been taking notes, haven't you?"

"It's just obvious stuff that I'm sure everyone sees."

"You'd be surprised what people overlook."

Cameron wondered what he meant. She wondered what had happened with his broken engagement, but he didn't seem to be in a hurry to tell her the details. And she didn't feel she should ask. He'd tell her when he was ready.

The waitress stopped by for their order. Cameron decided on green curry with chicken. Seth ordered a garlic pork entrée.

"Maybe I should have ordered the pork." Cameron closed her menu. "It sounds wonderful."

"We can share. I'd love to try the curry. I've never had it before."

"I like the way you think!"

Seth lifted his cup of water. "To new beginnings."

"To fresh starts." Cameron clinked her glass against his.

For the first time in a long time, she felt things were turning her way. This date with Seth would hopefully be one of many. Finally, the dark times would be fully in her past.

Chapter 9

"That was so much fun," Cameron laughed as she and Seth walked through the front door of the inn. "I haven't gone mini golfing since I don't know when. And I can honestly say I've never played golf like that before."

"The black lights certainly made it interesting."

"Especially when I hit the ball out of the—what do you call them, rails? Guards? Whatever. You know what I'm talking about—the border that frames the fake, green grass stuff?" She motioned with her hands. "I mean, how are you supposed to find the thing in the dark?"

"Oh yeah. When we were at the seventh hole?" Seth chuckled. "That was great. I haven't laughed that hard in years. The expression on your face—it was nice of them to give you another ball."

"I'm so glad you found me amusing. Yeah, I'm scared to know how many balls are over in that corner in the dark. A person could break their neck trying to find the right one."

"I'm sorry that storm came up and ruined the other plans I had, but the indoor mini golfing worked in a pinch."

"It more than worked. Spontaneous plans are the best kind. I think we should take the youth group over there soon. Can you imagine how amusing that would be?"

"Good point. I'll run it by Caleb." Seth's lazy smile made Cameron's heart skip a beat. "He loves doing stuff like that with the kids."

"Poor Josie. After she marries him, she's destined to a life of parenting a dozen or more kids at any given time. I'm including Caleb in that number."

"I won't tell him you said that. And from what I understand, she embraces the thought of having so many kids around."

"Very true. She loves children."

Seth leaned against the inn's closed front door. "How about you?"

"Hmm?"

"Do you love children?"

She smiled. "I wouldn't deliver babies if I didn't love them."

"So you want some kids of your own?"

"Absolutely. I'd love children someday. In the meantime, like Josie, I enjoy working with the youth and playing with the babies I deliver."

His nod and smile implied that he liked her answer.

Cameron wondered if they'd have the awkward after-date moment when neither person knew how to say good night. She'd never ended a date at a public arena like the bed-and-breakfast, which added another element of indecision. Should she say good night and walk away? She wondered if he planned to kiss her. And did she even want him to?

Maybe she should suggest they go back to the kitchen and have a snack—that would bring them some privacy and would be a bit more like coming home from a date to a normal setting. But then they'd be right outside Ginny's door. No matter how she analyzed the situation, each scenario felt awkward.

Or maybe she was overthinking it. She glanced up at Seth.

He gawked at her, a funny expression on his face. "Did you come to a conclusion?"

"A conclusion?" She willed her face to look blank.

"I lost you there for a minute. Looked like you were playing a mental game of tug-of-war. What was the winning verdict?"

"Don't-wanna-talk-about-it." She mumbled.

"Tell me." He nudged her. "Maybe I can give some input that'll help."

Mortified didn't begin to cover the emotion she was feeling at the moment. A flush rolled over her skin. She was surprised the front hall wasn't glowing. Maybe a better move would be to not dwell on kissing Seth at all and let nature take its course. "I'm good."

"Well, if you're sure." He glanced over at the entry table. "Hey—it looks like someone left a note for one of us." He walked over, picked it up, and skimmed it. "It's for you. Mandy isn't feeling so hot and wants you to stop by before you go to bed."

"And here I stand chatting. I'll get my bag and go right up. She's close enough to her due date that I don't want to take any chances. She's ready to go at any moment."

"Um, when you say *go*, you mean *go* as in 'go to the hospital,' right?"

Cameron laughed. "I mean *go* as in 'have a baby.' If we have time to go to the birthing center or hospital—yes, that would be optimal."

"If?" Seth ran a hand through his hair. "I'm thinking there might have been a lack of communication somewhere between, 'Can the girls stay here at the inn while we're working on fixing the issues at the center?' and 'We're going to be delivering babies at the inn.' That isn't really the kind of draw or publicity we're going for."

Men. "You have to admit, it's a unique advertising angle."

"Not the kind of unique I'm looking for, thank you very much."

"Relax. The chances of Mandy going into active labor that fast with a first baby are slim to none."

"The slim part has me a bit worried."

Cameron snickered. "Since she didn't text or call my cell, it probably isn't that big of a deal. I'm sure it'll be fine. I'll get my bag, and we'll check 'er out."

"I'll follow you so I can pace in the hall. Every mom-to-be deserves to have someone in their corner, wearing a hole in the carpet, *outside* the arena where the event is taking place. Far, far outside."

"You're such a trouper," Cameron snorted as she hurried past and headed for the suite to get her bag. Ginny's door was closed, and a low-wattage light burned on the end table beside the couch.

Seth waited outside the kitchen door. They hurried up the hall. Cameron stopped at the bottom of the stairs. Seth cupped her elbow. "Is something wrong?"

"Not really. I just suddenly realized how tired I am now that I'm looking at all those stairs."

"We only have two flights. I've seen you jog up them many times before."

"I can promise you I wasn't feeling this tired then."

"Too late a night for you?" He teased. "I didn't peg you to be the type to turn into a pumpkin at ten."

"I don't turn into a pumpkin." She started up the stairs to shut him up. She felt like she was wearing lead boots. The medical bag felt like deadweight in her hands. *Why was she so exhausted?*

Seth swung the bag from her hand and supported her elbow. She envisioned him hooking her to a lift machine and hoisting her up the stairs. The image made her happy. That's how exhausted she was. If only it could come true.

She needed to talk to Josie. Maybe she was having some kind of backlash, since she hadn't really grieved Jim's death.

"For future reference, you do know we have an elevator, right?"

We. Such a beautiful word. His words sank in. "Wait. We have an *elevator*?" She stopped midstep and stared at him. "How come I didn't know this before now?"

"I guess no one ever thought to tell you. The flyer we send to guests lists it with the amenities, but since we haven't had any guests who needed to use it, I guess it just never came up."

"How about when I had to carry all my bags and boxes from my car to my room when I moved in? That might've been a good time to enlighten me."

"Hmmm. I don't think I was here when you moved in. Josie and Mandy both used it."

"Glad you decided to let me in on that little secret.

I'll file it for future reference." Cameron resumed the climb.

Seth stopped her on the second floor and led her to an ornate door. He motioned to it with an elaborate sweep. "The elevator." He pushed a button that was nicely concealed in the carved wood decorations.

"I would have never known. It looks like a regular door."

She caressed the woodwork. "I can see where you'd rather not have garish silver elevator doors marring the effect. You do beautiful work."

"Thank you." He beamed as the door slid quietly open, and he ushered her inside. The car was small and intimate. This would be the perfect place for a spontaneous first kiss, but Seth carried her cumbersome bag and it would be hard to segue from architecture to a romantic kiss in the few seconds it was taking them to reach the third floor. And with that thought, she'd left spontaneity and moved into overly-thought-out. Though she had to admit she was game.

Seth looked at her again, but not with an "I want to kiss her" kind of look, more like a concerned "There she goes zoning out again" kind of look.

She needed to fill the silence. "So the door opposite the kitchen and up the hall a few feet—the one you stood in front of while you were waiting for me just now—I take it that isn't a storage closet?" she asked dryly.

"Nope."

"So we could have taken the elevator straight up."

"Yep."

"Ya learn something new all the time."

The door slid open, and they stepped out into the quiet hall on the third floor. Light from a television flickered through Mandy's open door at the far end. They walked toward it, but Seth hung back while Cameron peeked inside the room. Josie sat in the armchair. Mandy lounged on the bed.

"Hey girls. Looks like a slumber party in here. Everything okay?"

"Cam!" Mandy pushed herself higher on the bed. "We've been waiting up for you."

Josie hit the mute button on the remote.

"We saw the note. It's only ten o'clock. What's with the 'waiting up'? Since when do you go to bed this early?"

"Since tonight. I didn't feel so good. Josie suggested I try to sleep. I couldn't. I can't get comfortable. Nothing helps."

"That certainly sounds like the early stages of labor. We'll check you out and see what's going on."

Mandy got an impish look on her face. "First things first. How did the date go? Did Seth kiss you good night? Was it a good kiss? Dish!"

Cameron didn't think she could blush any more deeply than when Seth had asked about her wayward thoughts in the entry. She was wrong. "You could ask him yourself. Since he's standing right behind me."

"Oh hey, Seth." Mandy threw a hand against her mouth and giggled, showing no remorse at all. "My bad."

Against her better judgment, Cameron looked over her shoulder. Just as she thought, Seth stood behind her, grinning, his arms folded across his chest.

He looked like a warrior with his longish hair framing his face. The dim light gave him a dangerous and mysterious edge. And she couldn't help but notice the way the lighting accentuated his very, very handsome features. His amused eyes met hers with something akin to a dare. Did that mean he *wanted* to kiss her? She had a bit of trouble tearing her eyes away from his. One thing was clear—there was no way Mandy had missed seeing Seth in the hall behind Cameron when she asked about the date. She'd throttle the girl as soon as she made sure both mama and baby were okay.

Seth could only imagine the mutinous thoughts that were passing through Cameron's mind after Mandy's not-so-innocent question. Mandy had made solid eye contact with Seth before bringing up the date and the kiss. If she'd wanted to see Cam squirm, she'd gotten the intended result. He wasn't so sure Mandy should irritate her midwife at this point in her pregnancy—if ever.

Several emotions passed through Cameron's eyes before she tore her gaze away from his and turned to her patient.

The funny thing was, for all Seth's bluster about not wanting a relationship, the idea of kissing Cameron was one he could fully embrace. He set the thought aside as she waved him into the room.

"Mandy, I'm going to take your blood pressure, and as long as you lay still, you can ask Seth all the questions you want about our date."

Panic replaced Seth's smugness. "Um, I don't want to intrude on such a personal situation. I think I'll call it a night."

"Oh no, Seth." Josie shifted on the chair. "I think Cameron has a great idea. She'll be busy checking Mandy's blood pressure, the baby's heartbeat—all those noninvasive things—and you'll provide a wonderful diversion for Mandy. For all of us, as a matter of fact."

Josie's dark eyes sparkled with anticipation. She was much too eager to put him under the microscope.

He had no clue why he'd stumbled up here. He'd willingly let himself be led to the slaughter. The idea of squeezing out a few more minutes in Cameron's company had sounded good at the time. Now, he'd invaded women's territory. Mandy's room exploded with bright colors, flowery decorations, and girlie things. Josie had apparently been busy helping the teen settle in. The entire setting that spread out before him looked like something out of one of the chick flicks he avoided like the plague.

"Come." Josie patted the chair beside hers. "Make yourself comfortable. Take a load off."

Yep, just as he'd thought—like a lamb to the slaughter.

He didn't intend to be the main event in their late-night entertainment. Mandy was welcome to that role.

"No thanks. I think I'd better go." Seth almost tripped in his hurry to get out the door. He bypassed the elevator and jogged down the stairs two at a time. Josie's and Mandy's laughter chased him. Cameron was probably grinning. He knew her well enough to know that, irritated or not, she would have found his fast retreat amusing.

He didn't slow until he'd jogged through the storm to reach his place out back. He shut the door and leaned against it, breathing hard. He surveyed his masculine room and let out a breath of relief. He was safe. He'd entered his manly place of refuge.

Raindrops ran down his hair and onto his face as he paced the small room. He didn't care. He returned to the door, bolting the lock in place. He wouldn't put it past Josie and Mandy to chase him down. Getting the scoop apparently even displaced imminent childbirth.

He admitted that the only person he wanted to chase him down at the moment was Cameron. *Hmph.* Best intentions aside, she was getting under his skin.

He doubted they'd get information out of her. She didn't seem the type to kiss and tell. Not that they'd even had time to share a good-night kiss. He had half a mind to surprise her by waiting up in the kitchen. That would throw her for a loop.

A lightning bolt struck nearby, and the resounding thunder shook the windows. Maybe the kiss could wait. He'd find a way to get her alone, soon, and he'd give her a kiss she could talk about.

Whether she chose to or not would be up to her.

Cameron wrapped the blood pressure cuff around Mandy's arm. "Not a cool idea to annoy the person who has full control of your pain relief during labor, Mandy."

"You wouldn't withhold my pain meds." Mandy gulped. "Would you?"

Mandy glanced over at Josie.

Josie just shrugged.

"Cam…?"

"Nah. Of course not—I just wanted to see you squirm for a minute. But I can't believe you went there. You knew Seth was behind me." She adjusted the cuff. "Stop wiggling."

"I knew you wouldn't tell me anything. I was looking for a reaction."

"Did you get one?"

"I did." She grinned.

Cameron jotted a note on the pressure and listened to Mandy's heart. "Are you having contractions?"

"Not so much contractions, but my back keeps hurting."

"That could also be a sign of early labor." She took Mandy's pulse. "And what reaction did you get?"

"Great responses on both of your faces. You both looked guilty. And then he gave you that look that said he wouldn't mind kissing you one bit."

The girl was way too perceptive. "He—he, um…" Cameron cleared her throat. "He didn't look at me like that."

"Josie?" Mandy turned back to her. "Referee this part, will you?"

"Unfortunately, I'm over here in the corner, and I couldn't see his expression until he stepped into the room. I apparently missed all the good stuff that happened before we chased him off."

Mandy's face fell. "I ruined your date, didn't I? I should have left the note on your bed so you wouldn't get it until the date was officially over."

Cameron bent down and gave her a hug. "It was already over, pumpkin. You didn't ruin a thing. Taking care of you is what I do. It's my passion."

"Well, it wouldn't hurt if you had a little passion of the other sort in your life. I'm telling you, I could read the signs. For a minute there I thought Seth was going to march in and kiss you on the spot."

Cameron blushed. Again. "That would be a bit public for me for a first kiss."

"Aha! So he didn't kiss you. But judging by your blush, you'd like him to."

"Mandy, stop!" Cameron walked to the door and stuck her head out, looking left and right.

"Did you think he'd sneak back to listen to us gossip about him?"

"I certainly hope not."

"Leave her alone, Mandy. Let's focus on you." Josie was gentle but firm as she redirected the conversation.

Cameron mouthed *thank you* and returned her attention to her patient "So, you think you can sleep now? You can call for me if anything new comes up or if things intensify. Definitely call me if you start having contractions or if the backache gets worse."

Josie stood and stretched. "I think I'll stay in here for the night. If you don't mind sitting here with her for a few minutes, Cam, I'll go get my things."

"I'd love nothing more than a few minutes to settle into that chair you just vacated."

"Have at it."

Cam didn't have to be asked twice. She snuggled into the soft, warm chair and closed her eyes.

"I don't exactly need a babysitter," Mandy grumbled.

Josie mussed her hair. "We know you don't, but we like to watch out for you all the same. Humor us."

"You both need to get a life."

"We're working on it, young'un. Give us time."

Cameron looked at her friends and knew she'd made the right choice in coming to Lullaby. This is what she lived for. Friendship and babies. She couldn't wait until Mandy's baby made his or her appearance. Though she'd delivered babies since she'd arrived, she hadn't built a relationship with the families. She'd assisted and covered for Doc when he needed her, she saw patients in his clinic, but she hadn't built the bonds she was building with her Lullaby girls.

Each Lullaby Landing birth would be a special delivery.

Josie reentered the room with full arms. She dumped the load on the foot of the other bed.

Mandy leaned over to look. "Are you moving in permanently?"

Josie perused her pile. "No. Why?"

"You have enough things there to last a week!"

"I have my robe and blanket. My favorite pillow, a book, and a candle. My beauty supplies for the morning. An overnight bag in case you go into labor and we have to go to the birthing center. Some, um, rations in case the labor drags on."

"Rations?"

"Sure. Candy. Gum. Nuts. Bottled water. A couple of magazines. Just the basics."

Cameron laughed. "Looks like you'll be comfy as can be while I'm working hard to deliver a baby."

"Hey, somebody's got to keep their strength up."

"On that note, I'll leave you to your slumber party," Cameron said. "I'm off to bed before I turn into a pumpkin." She smiled a secret smile when she remembered that Seth had said those very words to her on their way upstairs. "And it'd do you two well to make it an early night—if you can call it that—and hit the rack, too. We have a baby to birth."

Josie nodded. "Going to bed right now, aren't we Mandy?"

Mandy reached for the light.

Josie hurried to move her things from the foot of the bed while Cameron walked out the door and closed it behind her. Her tiredness clung to her. She hoped she'd have a solid night's sleep before waking to deliver any babies.

Chapter 10

Early the next morning, Cameron jerked from a deep sleep, and her eyes popped wide open in horror. She tried to ignore the thoughts that pressed into her mind.

I'm pregnant.

It wasn't so much a question as a statement. So much for sleeping in. Her mind was racing and wouldn't let her go back to sleep.

Could it really be true? The thoughts came hard and fast. *Nausea. Exhaustion—she was always tired. The fact that her pants wouldn't fasten. That final weekend with Jim—the last-ditch effort to save their marriage.*

Cameron thought she'd been having a nightmare when she woke up with goose bumps, but the question had plagued her sleep.

Was it really possible that she could be pregnant?

Of course not. It wasn't possible. Well, it was possible, but it wasn't what she wanted. Was it? She'd always wanted a baby. But not now. Not like this. In the past, when she'd pictured herself pregnant, she'd always imagined she'd share the experience with a loving husband, and her baby would know the unconditional love of a doting father.

That brought her to the next concern. She was a midwife, for Pete's sake. How could she have missed the signs? How could she not have noticed? She must be well into her second trimester. Sure, she'd been busy and had experienced a lot of changes recently, but four months of pregnancy as a midwife without knowing? She felt like an idiot.

She thought of her clients. She had no right to complain. They would be alone as new mothers, too, but that didn't change the fact that they were expecting and under way worse circumstances than Cameron. Cameron had a career, a steady income, an inheritance.

She exhaled a shaky breath. She may be a single mom, but she wasn't really alone. She had friends, support, and a strong relationship with God.

The thoughts pummeled her, fast and relentless. How would she manage a baby on her own with the crazy hours she kept? She loved her job, and while she could afford to quit and live on her bank account, she didn't want to. The girls needed her. She needed them.

And what would everyone think? She hadn't even told anyone that she'd been married! Only a select few on the hiring committee and a few close friends knew her situation. Now she'd have so much explaining to do, and on such a private topic! How could she explain that she had been married, that she was getting a divorce, but months ago, before the divorce was finalized, the husband passed away…and oh, by the way, now she was pregnant with that husband's baby?

She shook her head. Maybe it would be easier to leave town.

And Seth. Her heart fell. What would this do to her budding relationship with him? Surely he'd run like the sane man he was. But she didn't want him to. She was just coming to realize how different he was from Jim, and now the rug had been pulled out from under her.

It was like Jim had the last laugh from the grave. By giving her a baby—the very thing she'd asked for, that she'd wanted for so long—he'd mess up everything she had going now.

"Jim has nothing to do with this blessing. This blessing comes from Me."

The quiet voice inside her head calmed her to an extent. It was true. Babies were always blessings. Wasn't that her favorite thing to spout to the girls? To all her patients? They might not always arrive in the best of circumstances. Sometimes their parents made poor choices and didn't do things God's way. But they were always blessings from God, every single one of them.

"This blessing comes from Me."

Was God reassuring her about her predicament? She felt that must be what He was trying to tell her. If God had His hand in this, good would come of it. She was sure of that. *"And we know that in all things God works for the good of those who love him, who have been called according to his purpose."*

Tears welled. She didn't understand why she'd prayed for a baby for all those years, always to have Jim say no, just to have her prayers answered after the fact. Cameron just had to be still and wait to see what God had planned. He did work in mysterious ways, so trying to figure it out wouldn't do anything but cause additional frustration. She'd find out in His perfect timing.

When she could no longer stand the questions and *what-ifs*, she got up and padded to the bathroom. She stood before the full-length mirror, lifted her sleep shirt, and turned sideways, studying her profile. A soft roundness replaced her previously flat stomach and further proved her theory. How could she have missed so many signs?

"Sometimes the hardest things to see are the things you aren't looking for in the first place."

Eloise loved to say that. She said Cameron wasn't naive, but positive—meaning Cameron didn't look for the bad or negative in people, or in things. Instead, she focused on the good. Eloise had said this several times when reassuring Cameron about Jim's personality. The saying especially applied to Jim's shortcomings and Cameron's blindness to them—his abusive personality, his coldness, what her future would be like if she married him. She hadn't seen the signs.

But he'd been careful to hide them.

Cameron hadn't been expecting a pregnancy, so why would she look for the signs?

Her black bag contained pregnancy tests. She walked into the bedroom to retrieve one, her footfalls like lead. She'd held the plastic sticks in her hands many, many times before, but never had she looked at it from this angle. This test would lay out the future in a way she hadn't expected. Would the test result bring relief? Or would it bring panic?

Her mind reeled. She felt a new empathy for the girls in her care. She couldn't imagine the terror a young girl felt over telling her parents or the father of the baby. How scary it would be to have no support system or job or even a place to live. Lullaby Landing was created to help those girls, but word had to get out before they knew to come.

Cameron followed the directions on the test and hopped in the shower, sure she'd go insane if she waited moment by moment to see the results.

The warm water soaked her hair. She closed her eyes and let it run over her face. *Lord, help me to see a positive test as the blessing it's meant to be. I know babies are blessings. If You choose to give me this blessing, I'll do my best to see it as the gift that it is.* She turned around and let the water ease the tension in her back. *Also, help me not to be disappointed if the test is negative.*

Disappointed? She wiped her face and opened her eyes. Where did *that* come from?

It took all of her willpower not to jump out of the shower and peek at the tiny stick that rested on the product box on the counter. She suddenly wanted to see what it said. A ping of hope started to grow inside her, a tiny flicker that grew into a full-blown flame.

A baby wouldn't be a negative to her new start— it would be a positive end to the old life, a wonderful start to the new.

Instead of jumping out to see if the little window said negative or pregnant, she forced herself to take the time to calmly wash and condition her hair, to soap her body, and to rinse, just like any other day. The results wouldn't change just because she hurried through her shower.

But it wasn't an ordinary day. The results on the cheap plastic stick across the room had the power to change her life.

She reached for a towel and wrapped one around her hair and another around her body. She slowly stepped from the shower. Slower yet, she walked toward the counter, her feet cold on the tile floor. Her trepidation was palpable, but suddenly she realized she was dreading a negative result more than a positive. The tiny seed of hope that had sprouted inside her suddenly bloomed into full-fledged desire.

She wanted a baby. It wouldn't matter that the baby was conceived with a man she no longer loved. A husband who had died. What mattered was that something good had come from the difficult marriage.

The little test window showed Pregnant in bright pink.

Cameron's legs went weak. She sat on the dressing-table stool. *Pregnant.* Wanting it and seeing it were two different things. Her emotions hadn't caught up with her pinging thoughts.

At this moment an ultrasound would show her a baby complete with flailing arms, kicking legs, and perfect little features. Within the next two weeks she'd be able to tell if she carried a son or a daughter.

A knock sounded on her bedroom door.

Cameron jumped. She stood, a bit unsteady, and walked to answer, clutching the stick behind her back.

"I thought I heard the shower when I came to check on Ginny—" Eloise stared. "Chile, you better sit down. You look like you done seen a ghost."

"El." Cameron couldn't get anything else past her lips. She lowered herself to the edge of the bed and held out the stick without a word.

El looked at it, confused, then clutched her chest and sat on the bed beside her. "Oh my goodness. I've seen those on TV. We didn't have them back in my day, but…" She grabbed Cameron by the wrist to hold it still. "Stop waving that thing in my face and let me take a peek. I'm guessing by your shell-shocked expression that it's positive."

Cameron squeaked out a "yes."

"I knew it!" She threw her arms around Cameron, pulling her into a big hug. "Congratulations, Mama. I suspected last night when your clothes wouldn't fasten. We gonna have ourselves a baby!"

Ginny called out from the other room. "What's all the excitement about?"

Cameron clutched Eloise with a death grip. "Don't tell her!"

"Hon, the whole world's gonna know soon enough. You ain't gonna be hidin' that belly much longer."

"I know, but I need time to come to grips myself before the whole world knows."

"Fair enough. I know it must be a scary prospect to face motherhood alone like this."

"It is."

Eloise studied her. "We don't have to say anything right now. You'll know when the time is right." She stood and tucked a strand of hair back into the towel. "For now, why don't you get up and get ready for the quilting group? I'll go tend to Ginny." Eloise walked to the door and hesitated, her features crinkled with concern. "Will you be okay?"

"I'll be fine." Cameron's forced smile felt more like a grimace. "We'll talk more later."

After Eloise left, Cameron continued to sit on the edge of the bed.

A baby.

She glanced around the room. She had plenty of room for a bassinette, but it wouldn't be right to bother Ginny with a newborn's cries. She'd need to move. Would Eloise and Alfie come with her to her new place? They seemed to love it here at the inn, and they were helpful to Seth and Ginny. She didn't want to move alone.

Hysterical laughter bubbled from deep within. Why was she worried about such mundane details? She was having a *baby*. She was excited, she was scared, she didn't know what the future held…. And yet, a sense of peace enveloped her. The *"peace of God, which transcends all understanding."* She wrapped her arms around her stomach and smiled.

First things first. She needed to make an appointment with Dr. Thomas.

Fortunately she ate well and exercised. There wasn't much she'd have to do differently. She'd need to switch from her regular vitamins to prenatals.

She wanted to hop in her car and head to the clinic for an ultrasound. No one was there today. She'd have the place to herself.

But she couldn't. Ginny was counting on her to set up the sitting room for the quilting group. Life continued all around her. She stood up and got dressed.

The ultrasound would have to wait.

"Cameron, the ladies from the quilting group will be here soon," Ginny called from the suite. "How are the arrangements coming along? Is the room ready?"

Cameron, still walking on cloud nine, winked at Mandy and went to reassure her older friend. Seth was busy in the kitchen, making, as he called it, his "signature hors d'oeuvres" for the ladies, whatever that meant.

Cameron peeked into the suite. Ginny sat on the couch, resting, with her quilting supplies ready and waiting on the cushion beside her. She glanced up as

Cameron stood in the opening between the sitting area and the kitchen.

"You look radiant today. Your date with Seth last night must have suited you."

"I had a really good time." Cameron grinned. It took everything she had not to rest her hand on her growing belly.

"I'm glad to hear it. Seth is a wonderful man. And I don't think he could find a better woman than you to spend time with." Ginny looked at her while plucking at a loose thread on the cushion. "I have several of the ladies praying for the both of you."

"Lord knows we can always use extra prayers." Cameron again resisted rubbing her hand on her stomach.

"Well, these are very *specific* prayers, if you know what I mean." She met Cameron's eyes. "I'd love to have you as my niece."

"Ginny!" Cameron glanced over her shoulder at Seth, who was busy at the far end of the kitchen. Thankfully he hadn't heard.

"Well, it's true."

"And I'd love to have you as an aunt—that would be the most wonderful thing ever. But I don't want to rush things. Things are—difficult—at the moment."

"Aren't they always? But it's easier to face difficulties when you have someone you love at your side. The two of you can bolster each other."

One of us certainly needs bolstering.

The thing was, Cameron wasn't sure if Seth would want to be the one giving support in this situation. "We'll let God take care of that."

"I agree. And it never hurts to help things along— which is why I have the ladies praying."

Cameron wasn't sure how to handle the next few

hours, let alone her future. Was it fair to lead Seth on? She was sure he'd want to know about something like this. But how to tell him? *Hey, I had a great time last night. I'd love to go out on another day. By the way, how do you feel about dating pregnant women?*

It was enough to chase even the stoutest of friends away, and they'd barely reached friend status. She decided to change the subject. "Thank you. I appreciate the prayers. As for your original question, we're doing fine with the preparations. We have the sitting room set up exactly as you requested. Everything's ready but the food."

"Thank you, dear."

Seth appeared at her elbow. "The hors d'oeuvres will be ready momentarily."

Ginny smiled. "Oh good. I appreciate it, Seth. Eloise deserved some time off."

"He all but shoved me out the back door!" Eloise stood on her tiptoes to see over Seth and Cameron. "I had to sneak back in to see how he was doing."

"He's doing great," Seth said.

"Back to your stations." Ginny laughed and waved them out of the room. "Eloise, you're supposed to be taking a break."

"I am. I just laid my quiltin' supplies on the kitchen table so I could say hi to you. I'm so excited about joinin' this group! I can't wait to see all the works in progress and to figure out what I'll be makin'."

"We're excited to have you. All my friends have heard me rave so much that they can't wait to meet you. Ethel said she's coming early just so she can have some time to get to know you before the others arrive."

"Then I'd best be gettin' out there to greet her!"

"No need. She'll find you when she gets here. No

one knocks at the inn. They'll mosey back here as they arrive."

Cameron smiled as she and Eloise walked through the kitchen arm in arm. Seth had disappeared and was nowhere to be seen.

"How's the baby mama doin'?" Eloise whispered.

"Does 'terrified' give you any indication?"

"You're gonna do great. Don't you be gettin' yourself all het up over things. It ain't good for the baby."

"Oh my."

"You ain't goin' through this alone, you know. Al and I will be by your side no matter where you go. No way I'm lettin' anyone else get their hands on this wee one. It's our first and only grandchild."

"Oh Eloise, do you mean it?" Cameron sighed with relief.

"Of course I mean it. Who else would be capable of takin' care of the young'un while you're at work? I knew we was brought here for a reason, and I think that reason was to help you with this little one."

"And here I thought you came to be close to me."

"You know we did. You're a package deal. We're here for the both of you."

She gave Eloise a hug. "You have no idea how happy I am to hear that. I've been trying to figure out the details since this morning."

Eloise leveled her with a glare. "I told you not to be worryin' none. You gonna be this difficult through the whole pregnancy?"

"I tried not to overthink things, but how could I not? It's a lot to take in. The not-worrying thing is easier said than done. But with you and Al by my side, I'll be fine. I'm so happy you're here!"

"So am I. I didn't have any friends in Kansas City.

Al and I were always busy with one thing or another at the house. We didn't have time to socialize. Here—it's like we have no choice but to socialize! There's always somethin' fun going on."

"Next week we'll start back to church. Ginny said after the past three weeks in physical therapy she's been released to go. You'll meet so many more friends there."

Seth entered the kitchen and stepped past them to pull a tray from the oven. The savory scent of minced onions mixed with seasoned pork drifted through the kitchen as he set the platter on the stove. He slid a tray of sliced cookie dough into the oven and set the timer.

Cameron peeked over his shoulder. "It smells wonderful."

"Of course it does. I'm a whiz in the kitchen."

"Then why is Ginny always the one doing all the cooking?"

"Mostly because she insists. If you haven't noticed, she's kind of a warden when it comes to the kitchen."

Ginny's voice piped in. "I heard that! I might have a cast on my leg, but my hearing is just fine."

Cameron didn't even bother to hide her laughter.

Seth rolled his eyes. "I kind of expected that, Aunt Ginny. The door to your suite is open, and you're about two feet from the opening. I wasn't trying to be discreet, just factual. It's all true, you know."

"Not that I've seen." Eloise hovered on the other side of him. She bumped him with a shoulder. "Ginny's been as tolerant as can be with me. She's given me free reign in there to do as I please."

"That's because you're her lifeline. She couldn't be mean to you if she wanted to be."

"And with Ginny laid up, *I* have to keep you in line."

Eloise blustered. "So don't go messin' with me or the kitchen while it's on my watch."

"Yes ma'am." Seth slapped Cameron's hand with his spatula as she reached around him for puff pastry.

"Ow!"

"Those are for the ladies!"

"I bed your pardon. I'm a lady in case you haven't noticed!"

"Oh, I've noticed."

Eloise snickered.

"I didn't mean it that way." Seth raised an eyebrow at her then turned to Cameron. "You'll get your share—when the snacks are served."

"My stomach's doing funny things. I thought maybe a bite or two would help calm it." She dared a peek at Eloise.

Eloise raised her eyebrow.

Cameron knew it was an understatement, but she couldn't help it. Her stomach was churning, and food seemed to help.

Seth leveled her with a look. "That's the best excuse you could come up with?"

"It's the truth!"

He sighed. "Here, take a plate and grab yourself something to eat. Tea sandwiches are on a platter in the fridge, mini quiches warming in the holding oven. Fruit and veggies over there on the counter. It pays to know the chef."

Distracted, she focused on his mouth. The mouth she'd wanted to kiss the night before. Before she had a chance to take the plate from him, he filled it up with snacks for her.

Cam took the plate and squeezed a few more appetizers on the empty spot.

Seth shook his head. "How you stay so slim is beyond me."

"Hey!" Cameron yelped.

"Seth!" Ginny called from the suite. "You be nice."

"I am being nice." He leaned close to Cameron's ear. "You owe me. Just remember this moment in the future when I ask for something."

She hoped there would be a future after he found out her news. "I'll try. My memory can be fickle, depending on what you need. Just sayin'." She gave him a saucy grin and headed for the table. "Besides, I'm doing you a favor. Consider me your personal, royal taste tester. You wouldn't want to put out a bad product. The ladies would never let you live it down."

"I appreciate your thoughtfulness."

"Thank you." She pointed her fork at him. "Surely you know that those ladies can be ruthless if you cause them distress."

"I'm not sure you have to accentuate that comment with the word 'those' in this situation. From my experience, all ladies can be ruthless if you cause them distress."

Cameron wondered if he was thinking of his former fiancée. She wondered if she'd cause him distress when he found out about the pregnancy. She hoped not. To distract herself from the line of thoughts, she bit into a hot wing. "Oh! Hot. Spicy! I need water."

An icy glass of water magically appeared in her peripheral vision. "I figured you might need a drink when I saw that you chose that one."

"You could have warned me."

"You're right. I'm sorry. Did you like it? Is it good?"

"I love it. It's wonderful. I just didn't know I'd need a drink handy."

"All right, you've made your point. We need to warn the ladies that this appetizer is spicy. If you hadn't been my taste tester, I'd have forgotten that little detail."

"Any other disclaimers I ought to be aware of?"

"No. The rest of the appetizers are user-friendly."

Mandy rounded the corner from the hall. "Food! I'm so hungry I could eat a horse."

Everyone was silent. Cameron wondered if they, like her, were thinking that Mandy already looked like she had eaten a horse. Her almost-nine-month belly looked ready to pop.

Mandy eyed Cameron's food.

Seth rested his fists on his hips. "With you two coming in to raid the kitchen, I'm wondering if I've made enough."

They all stared at the multitude of platters lining the counter.

"I think you've made enough." Eloise deserved credits for stating the obvious without an undercurrent of sarcasm.

"I agree. It isn't like it's for a group of guys watching football or something," Cameron said between bites. "Just a few ladies who will keep their hands busy with their sewing."

"I see."

"So we need to start in now so you don't have too many leftovers."

"Speaking of creations, I've been thinking…." Mandy loaded the plate Seth handed her and headed for the seat next to Cameron. "Do you think the ladies would mind if I joined in? I'd like to make a quilt for the baby."

"I think they'd be delighted to have you as a part of

the group." Ginny rolled her wheelchair through the doorway of the suite.

"Aunt Ginny!" Seth hurried to her side. "You aren't supposed to be getting up and down without assistance. Why didn't you ask for help?"

"I did. Y'all couldn't hear me over all the cater-wauling."

"I'm sorry." Seth maneuvered her chair over to the table. He lowered himself next to her, his expression serious. "Are you okay? You didn't hurt yourself trying?"

"I'm fine, Seth." Ginny placed her hand on his. "I'm feeling stronger these past few days. I'm ready to get up and around. The physical therapy is helping a lot. We practice things like getting up and down, getting in and out of my chair. Wheeling it through doorways. I'm ready. I promise I won't do anything I'm not approved to do."

"Thanks, Aunt Ginny. I appreciate that."

She reached out and ruffled his hair. "I wouldn't want to make that pretty head full of hair you've got go prematurely gray."

"Speaking of gray"—Cameron jumped up from the table—"I have a box of colorful shirts that I thought everyone might want to go through for quilting squares. They're my grandfather's. I brought them down here because I couldn't bear to part with them. But I don't really have a use for them. Maybe some of you can use them in your quilts."

"Don't you dare go liftin' any heavy boxes!" Eloise snapped. "Seth, why don't you run along and get the box for Cameron? I'll watch over your snacks, Cammie."

Cameron sent Eloise a glare as she walked by. "Very subtle," she hissed.

Eloise shrugged as Cameron and Seth walked from the room.

Chapter 11

"Sailor, did you seriously just miss that shot?" Caleb's booming voice drowned out the raucous laughter of the other groups of teens as he razzed his daughter. The youth group had spread out over several of the nearby miniature golf holes, each group in its own stage of play. "Tell me. How on earth do you manage to miss a shot when your ball is teetering on the edge of the hole?"

Looking as perplexed as her father sounded, Sailor stared at him, exasperated, hands on hips. She'd been teasing him moments before she missed the shot.

Caleb winked at Cameron.

Cameron slapped her hand against her forehead.

"Seth? Remind me again why I suggested this as a youth event. I know how competitive the kids get, especially the grown-up ones." She sent Caleb a pointed look.

He pointed at himself and looked around, his face wreathed in innocence.

"Obviously you chose this activity because you love to see Sailor and her dad compete in high pressure situations." Seth teased. "Other than that, I'm not sure."

The kids at a nearby hole doubled over with laughter as one of the girls whacked the ball out of their area.

"Try not to break anything." Seth called out to them. "This is miniature golf, not a pro competition. Nice, gentle, steady shots please."

"I thought that *was* gentle." The girl quipped as she and several others went after her ball.

Sailor hit her ball into the cup and sent her dad a triumphant glare. "Beat that."

"I think I will. Let's see…. I have to make it in less than ten strokes, right? It'll be hard, but I'll see what I can do."

"Your sarcasm doesn't become you, Dad. I didn't take ten strokes. Josie, are you keeping score?"

"I am. You did it in three." Josie rolled her eyes at Caleb.

Sailor high-fived her boyfriend Brian after he scooped up her golf ball and joined her. She nudged her father as she waddled past him toward the walkway. "Try putting with a bowling ball stuck up your shirt. That might help you see the handicap I'm working under. My equilibrium is off. I can hardly see around my belly to locate my ball."

"Excuses." Caleb set his ball into place and took careful aim. He got a hole in one. "Yeah baby. Did you see that, Sailor? I'm showing you how it's done. Hey, come back here! Don't walk away!"

"I'm not walking away, Dad…. I'm just trying to make room for your ego. We'll never hear the end of this, Brian," Sailor grumbled. "Pressure is on, Josie. Make us proud."

"No pressure here." Josie set her ball into place. "I'm losing by a solid ten points. The upside of last place is that no one is breathing down your neck to take your spot."

"Hey, that's the attitude!" Caleb patted Josie's shoulder. "See how it is? There's a special place for everyone in this game."

Josie shook her head and concentrated on hitting the ball. It bounced off the guard and rebounded to jump over the hole. "Seriously?"

Caleb shook his head. "If you hadn't hit so hard, it would have gone right in. You'd have had a hole in one just like me and would have closed the gap between you and Sailor."

"Thanks for the commentary, Caleb."

"Anytime."

She hit it in on her second shot.

Cameron and Seth stood on the sidelines and enjoyed the show. Their group was up next. Cameron leaned close to Seth. The familiar scent of his earthy cologne tickled her senses. "Looks like Brian knows enough to stay out of this little family squabble."

"Smart boy." Seth crossed his arms and waited for Brian to take his turn. Brian made it in two shots.

"Well, Josie, look at the bright side," Caleb quipped. "You just closed in on Sailor by one point."

Sailor's giggle carried to Seth and Cameron as the foursome walked to the next hole.

"Looks like you're up." Seth motioned to Cameron. Allie and Mandy came over from a nearby bench to join them.

Cameron stayed in place. "I'm afraid to go after what

everyone just put Sailor and Josie through! I liked it better before we had the bottleneck. Maybe we can let them move ahead some before taking our turn?"

"Can't." Seth took her ball and placed it in position. "There are too many people coming up behind us. Ignore Caleb and go at your own pace. I doubt he'll pay attention anyway. He goofed off so much at this hole, the other groups moved ahead. They'll be busy on hole five."

Cameron returned her focus to their hole. She calculated the angle she needed to best avoid the spinning blades of the windmill that blocked her ball's path.

"Do you need to figure wind velocity and speed, too?" Seth drawled. "I can look them up on my phone."

Allie and Mandy giggled.

"We're indoors. I hardly think that figures in." She graced him with a glance. "And that's exactly the kind of comment I referred to a moment ago that makes me hesitate to take my turn."

"Just keeping it real." Seth winked at the two teens.

Cameron shifted her feet, trying to get comfortable in her stance. She adjusted her grip on the golf club and rolled her shoulders.

"Mandy's going to deliver her baby before you ever get around to hitting the ball."

"Seth! Hush. Let me concentrate." She readjusted her grip. She sensed rather than heard a presence behind her. "Whoever you are, I'm pretending you aren't crowding me while peering over my shoulder. You're just trying to break my concentration."

"It seems to be working." Brian's voice was inches from her ear.

"Aren't you supposed to be on the next hole?" Cameron blew out an exasperated breath. "Your group moved ahead, remember? You're done here."

"They said I was annoying them and sent me back to hang with you guys."

"Seth. I spoke too soon about Brian's tact."

"Yep."

Cameron glanced over at the fifth hole. Caleb, Josie, and Sailor waved.

"Thanks, guys."

"Anytime." Caleb leaned down to play his ball.

Cameron resumed her position. Shifted her feet. Adjusted her grip.

"And on hole four, we have Cameron Adams, trying to find her sweet spot." Brian stood to her left and held his golf club up to his mouth like a microphone. The girls at both holes clutching their sides with laughter. "Looks like she's going for the win, folks."

"Brian!" Cameron gave up and joined the laughter. She pointed toward the fifth hole with her club held in a menacing manner. "Go."

"But this looks way more interesting."

"Go. Now."

"I've never seen such technique."

"You heard the lady, Bri. Scoot." Seth sent him on his way.

Sailor and Cameron exchanged a look of long-suffering.

Cameron took advantage of the others' distraction and hit her ball. Like Caleb, she made a perfect hole in one.

"Yes!" She shouted, pumping her arm in the air. "Hole in one! What do you think of that, Brian?"

"Sorry, I was walking away from the shot—I had

my back to it—you told me to leave, remember?" Brian quipped.

"I remember." Cameron turned to Seth. "You saw it, right?"

"Nope, sorry. I was watching Brian to make sure he joined his group. I didn't want him to disturb you."

"Allie? Mandy? Did anyone see me make the shot?"

"Sorry." They said in unison. "Brian distracted us."

"I made a hole in one, my first and only, and no one witnessed it?"

"You could retry." Caleb called from the fifth hole.

"No, thanks." Cameron pouted. "It was beautiful."

"I'm sure it was." Seth ruffled her hair.

Cameron retrieved her ball and stepped to the side. Allie made her shot in four strokes. She hurried to the open space between holes four and five. Caleb had finished with hole five and was watching them.

"Hey, wait for me!" Mandy put her ball down and missed hitting it completely. The club swung clean over it.

Sailor and Allie fell against each other in gales of laughter.

"It's not funny." Mandy was laughing so hard she could hardly stand up. "Now I see what Sailor was saying. My belly completely obstructs the view of the ball."

"I told you. It's hard to see, isn't it?" Sailor sat on the nearby bench. "Take your time and step way back. It's awkward, but it works."

"You girls are a mess." Caleb shook his head. "I've never seen such drama in a game of mini golf."

"Then you've been missing out, Dad."

Josie sat down beside Sailor on the bench between the two holes.

Cameron watched Mandy's silliness. She'd come a

long way from the unkempt teen who'd kept everyone at arm's length.

"Looks like you folks are having a good time."

Cameron turned to see Dr. Thomas standing behind them with his wife. They were holding hands. Cameron would love to have a long-term marriage filled with such tenderness.

"Hi, Doc. Hi, Mrs. Thomas." Cameron motioned toward the kids. "As you can see, we brought the whole youth group along with us."

"You know better than to call me Mrs. Thomas, Cameron. How many times have you eaten at our table? It's Angie." She smiled and shook her head. "Brave souls, all of you adult leaders." She waved at Brit and Matt, who were trying to corral the middle schoolers at the ninth hole.

"Sorry," Cameron smiled. "I was trying to be proper for the kids' sake."

"We've worked with them enough that they call us by our given names, too. We don't stand on formality around here."

The teen girls' laughter drew their attention.

Dr. Thomas smiled at Mandy's antics. He waited until the girls quieted. "Still carrying that baby, Mandy?"

Mandy glanced up at him. "Not by any choice of my own. I'm more than ready for this little munchkin to arrive. I'm ready for the next step. He's late. The little guy seems to have a mind of his own."

"It's a boy?" Allie interrupted. "I didn't know you knew what you were having."

"I don't. I'm guessing."

"She has a fifty-fifty chance of getting it right," Doc Thomas laughed. He turned to Cameron. "We won't keep you. We've finished our game and are heading out for a nice quiet dinner."

Josie walked over to greet the Thomases.

"Have fun." Cameron waved them off. "And count your blessings that you got here before our crew did."

"We are, trust me." Angie agreed. "By the way, con-gratu-lations on your own news! I don't think I prop-erly congratulated you outside the office yesterday when you told me you were expecting. You could have knocked me over with a feather!"

"Um. Me, too." Cameron could barely speak. A roar like a freight train rushed through Cameron's ears. She'd forgotten to swear the doctor's wife to secrecy. The sounds of the mini golf course faded as she fo-cused on her friends' stunned expressions. "I felt the same way when I found out."

"I can tell by the look on your face." Angie came back over for a quick hug. "But you'll be a wonderful mom. That will be one loved little baby."

Josie stared at Cameron in shock. Behind the Thom-ases, Seth's face had gone white. His stance grew rigid with anger. Mandy and Allie looked at her in confusion.

Not noticing that they'd dropped a bombshell, the older couple waved and hurried out the door.

Cameron remained frozen in place. She'd only had a week to adjust to the news herself. Dr. Thomas had confirmed the test results the previous day. In the time since, she hadn't found the right way or place to tell Seth or anyone else. This wasn't how she'd wanted her friends to find out. She was glad that the other groups had moved on.

"Cam?" Josie stepped closer. "Is it true?"

Cameron nodded. She willed Seth to look at her. He wouldn't. His eyes dropped to her stomach. In response,

Cameron's hand rested protectively over her baby bump, which had grown profusely—or so it seemed at the moment—over the past week. She'd covered it with long cardigans and loose sweaters, but now it no longer mattered. Seth shook his head, his expression a mix of emotions. Shock, confusion, betrayal, and finally anger chased across his face. He might as well have physically kicked her, the impact was so intense. He shook his head, disgust the only remaining emotion.

Josie reached over and gripped Cameron's hand. Cameron fought the urge to cry out and bury her face on her friend's shoulder. Josie's warm fingers did nothing to dispel the icy cold that Cameron felt at Seth's rejection.

"Seth. Let me explain." Cameron's voice came out in a tortured whisper. She glanced at her friends. "I'll explain to everyone, but first I need to speak to Seth."

"I think we're beyond that." Seth handed Josie his golf club. "I need to get out of here. Josie, tell Caleb I'm sorry to run out on him."

"Seth, wait." Cameron reached for his arm, but he kept walking.

Josie motioned for Allie and Mandy to stay where they were. The girls nodded. Their eyes welled with tears.

Cameron ran after Seth. He'd reached his truck by the time she cleared the doors. Josie skidded to a stop beside her.

"It's too late. He's gone, Josie." Cameron's words came out on a sob. "I've made a mess of everything."

"Shush." Josie pulled her into a hug. "It's going to be okay."

Caleb came through the door. His jovial mood had

been replaced by concern. "Sailor suggested I come out here. What happened?"

Cameron was crying too hard to talk.

Josie turned to him. "Do you have your keys? Let's get her to the truck."

Caleb walked them to his vehicle and helped Cameron in. She sat facing them. Her friends formed a barrier to the outside world as they stood in the opening, protecting her from prying eyes.

Caleb turned to his fiancée. "Josie, what is it?"

"Cam?" Josie's voice was soft. "Do you want to tell him, or do you want me to?"

"I'm pregnant." Cameron buried her face in her hands. "I just found out myself, and I didn't know how to tell Seth. I didn't really know how to tell anyone. I've held back so much of my background that I don't even know where to begin."

Josie filled the gap when Cameron stopped talking. "Doc Thomas's wife congratulated her, and Seth overheard. He tore out of here without giving Cam a chance to explain."

"Oh no." Caleb looked over at Seth's empty parking spot and back to Cameron. "I'm really sorry, Cameron. I had no idea."

"I didn't e-either, not until last week." Cameron hiccupped. "I've been trying to come to terms with it on my own. I'm a midwife. I should have known sooner. And I know I should have told everyone, but I didn't want everyone judging me."

"Oh sweetie. You know we would have been here for you." Josie hugged her again.

"I kn-know. But I didn't know how to bring it up, and I was still reeling."

"I assume the baby is your ex's?" As a member of

the hiring committee, Caleb knew about Cameron's pending divorce at the time they'd hired her.

"Yes. We made an attempt at reconciliation r-right before I came here. It was a huge mistake. In September I called the a-attorney about the paperwork for the d-divorce." She broke down. "I found out Jim had died right after we separated in June. I'd pulled away from Eloise and Alfie. No one had been able to reach me to tell me."

"Cameron." A muscle worked in Caleb's jaw. "You didn't have to go through any of this alone. Didn't you know we'd be here for you?"

"I kn-knew. But it's all been so hard. I didn't want my new start to be clouded by the past."

"We wouldn't have judged you." He shook his head. "I mean, Cam, he was your *husband*. It's not like you had some fling and tried to hide it."

"It's a small town. I figured people would jump to conclusions about me. The whole situation was such a mess."

"And the baby?"

"I just figured it out last Saturday."

He pulled both Josie and Cameron into his firm bear hug. Cameron clung to him and cried like she hadn't cried in a long, long time.

"Cam? Josie? Caleb? Are you guys out here?" Brit's voice carried across the parking lot.

"We're over here. We'll be back in a few minutes. Can you hold down the fort?"

"Yep, Matt just wanted me to check and see where you'd gotten off to."

Cameron dropped her head to her hands. "I can't go back in there. Not right now."

"No, of course not." Josie turned to Caleb. "If I can

borrow the truck, I'll run Cameron home. You'd better head back inside and help Matt and Brit with the kids."

Caleb handed Josie the keys. "Cam—I'll be praying. Everything will be fine, you just wait and see."

"Seth hates me."

"I'm sure this feels like a slap in the face. He's thinking about what happened with his ex-fiancée." He made a dismissive wave with his hand. "I'll leave that for him to explain. When things get sorted out, I know he'll understand. Are you going to be okay?"

"I'll be fine. I just need to get out of here. I don't want to go back to the inn though. Not with Seth there."

Caleb thought for a moment. "Josie, why don't you take her back to my place? Hang with her there, and I'll catch a ride home with someone else. I'll meet you back there later."

"Thanks, Caleb." Josie gave him a quick kiss and hug. "Take your time. We need time to talk."

"I'll do damage control with the kids. I doubt Allie and Sailor said anything to anyone but me. They're good about stuff like this, and I'm sure they have empathy for you right now."

Cameron nodded. But the only thing she really cared about was Seth.

Judging by the look of anger on his face as he stormed out the door, she'd already lost him.

Chapter 12

When would he learn?

Seth took the turn a bit too fast, and his truck slid toward the graveled shoulder. He corrected the skid and adjusted his speed, willing himself to slow down. It wouldn't do anyone any good if he ended up in traction in the hospital. Especially with Aunt Ginny down for the count.

The past flashed before his eyes. It was bad enough his ex had duped him, but now he'd made the same mistake again with Cameron. Strangely enough, it hurt even more this time around. He'd thought Cam was different. She hadn't seemed the type to sleep around, but neither had his ex. He was obviously a poor judge of character, at least when it came to women.

Sylvia had seemed perfect for him. He'd been blinded by his emotions and let them carry him along. When she had shown up on the doorstep and announced she was pregnant by someone else, Seth had gladly let her walk away. They had agreed to wait until they were married to be intimate, but apparently she had been seeing someone else on the side.

But the emotions he'd felt with Sylvia didn't compare with the feelings he had for Cameron. He'd thought her the real deal.

Seth reached the inn's parking lot and slammed on his brakes, spewing gravel. He followed suit by slamming his truck door. He wanted to punch something— or someone. He stormed into the house and headed for his retreat out back. He was halfway through the kitchen when Aunt Ginny's voice stopped him in his tracks.

"Seth? Goodness gracious, son, what has you in such a dither?"

He closed his eyes and forced his breathing to slow. He should have walked around the house instead of passing through. He turned to see Aunt Ginny sitting in the dimly lit breakfast nook with Eloise. They were drinking tea.

"I didn't think you two would be up this late."

"Late?" Aunt Ginny glanced over at the clock on the microwave. "It's not even eight. We decided to have a bedtime snack. What are you doing home so early? I thought you kids would be out all evening."

"I thought so, too." Seth felt the tic in his jaw start up. His stomach churned. He stalked over to the ladies. "You really want to know why I'm home? I'm home because Cameron dropped a bombshell on us at the mini golf place. It's Sylvia all over again. I thought I'd learned that lesson."

Aunt Ginny's brow crinkled. "Seth, I don't know what's going on, but I can promise you Cameron isn't anything like Sylvia. That girl has a heart of gold, and she cares deeply for you."

"Does she? She has a funny way of showing it."

"Oh no." Eloise spoke for the first time. Her hand went to her heart. "She told you."

"*She* didn't tell me anything. I overheard Doc Thomas's wife congratulating her at the mini golf course." He studied Eloise's sad expression. "So, Eloise, you knew all along. Was I the only one in the dark? Aunt Ginny, did you know, too?"

"Apparently not, because I have no clue what either of you are talking about." Aunt Ginny looked from him to Eloise and back in the dim light.

"Cameron's pregnant, Aunt Ginny. Just like Sylvia."

His aunt's face crumpled, but Seth was too angry to worry about her feelings at the moment. She looked over at Eloise. "You knew about this?"

Eloise nodded. "She just found out last Saturday, right before the quilt meeting. She was trying to come to terms with the idea."

"Is it Jim's baby?"

"Of course." Eloise nodded again. "Cameron isn't the type to sleep around."

"Jim?" Seth sank into a chair. "Aunt Ginny, you knew she had another man in her life? You've been holding out on me." Heat shot through his limbs. His blood pressure must be in the scary range right now. He spoke through a clenched jaw. "You knew Cameron had someone on the side, and after all that I went through with Sylvia, you didn't think you should warn me?"

"It isn't what you think, Seth." She and Eloise exchanged glances. "I think you need to calm down and let Cameron explain from the beginning. She has to be devastated that you found out the way you did. Was anyone else around?"

"Josie, Caleb, and I, and a few of the teens."

"Oh, the poor dear." Aunt Ginny's eyes filled with tears.

Why was everyone feeling sorry for Cameron? She wasn't the one who had been deceived.

Or was she?

Seth exhaled slowly and tried to think. He had to admit he didn't know the full story. And he trusted these women. Aunt Ginny wouldn't defend Cam for being a liar or a hypocrite. His heartbeat slowed, and he felt the first root of remorse take hold.

Aunt Ginny dabbed at her eyes with a tissue. "She had to be beside herself."

He could picture the devastation on Cameron's face. "She was."

Eloise leaned forward. "So what happened? Didn't she try to explain?"

"She did. I walked out on her."

"Oh Seth." Eloise sighed and shook her head. "I know you don't understand, you haven't heard the full story, but Cameron has been dealing with such hard things since she moved here."

"I know she lost her grandfather, and I know she had to close his estate. But what's that have to do with Cameron having someone else's baby?"

"No, Seth." Eloise reached across the table and took Seth's hand in hers. "That's just a part of what she was dealing with. She lost her grandfather in the spring. The estate belonged to her husband."

Seth blanched. "Her husband?"

"I was his nanny from the time he was born. I stayed

on as housekeeper after he grew up. He was awful to her, Seth."

Seth's heart fell. He didn't want to hear this.

"He insisted on divorcing her, but the papers he was supposed to file never came. She called in September to find out what happened, only to be told he'd died in a car accident the day she moved down here."

"I had no idea."

"Of course you didn't."

"Why didn't she tell us?"

Aunt Ginny exchanged another glance with Eloise. "She wanted a fresh start. She didn't want to have to explain all her baggage when she was meeting people."

Eloise nodded. "Which made the pregnancy a bigger blow."

"This explains a lot." Seth ran his hands through his hair and tried to force his thoughts into some sort of order. He couldn't imagine how alone Cameron must have felt.

And how alone she must be feeling right now.

"I've really messed things up."

"You didn't know." Eloise gave his hand a squeeze. "She'll understand. She wanted to tell you, but she was waiting for the right time. She wasn't sure where she stood with you and didn't want to be presumptuous. You all had barely gone out when she figured out the signs. She didn't know how to tell you, or if dating her even mattered to you."

"Of course it matters. I wouldn't be dating her if I wasn't interested." He remembered their conversation at the Thai restaurant, all his blustering about just being friends. He slapped his forehead with his hand.

"She really got herself into a bind, didn't she?" Aunt Ginny asked softly.

Seth tried to choose his next words with care, but there was no way to dance around the subject. "If I might ask a tacky question, Eloise… If they were divorcing, how did she end up pregnant?"

"Jim was a master manipulator. He liked to be in control." She stared out the darkened window, frowning. "They were separated over a year when she decided to move down here and take the job. He couldn't stand the thought of her moving ahead without him, so he begged her to stay, to try again to make their marriage work." Eloise studied her teacup. "Cameron wanted to do the right thing. She agreed, and he tossed her aside like an unwanted rag."

"That's terrible. What a jerk."

"Yes. It is, and he was. He did a number on her confidence. She rallied when she came here, glad to know her past would stay in Kansas City. Instead, he managed to make a mess of things even from the grave."

"So to speak, anyway." Aunt Ginny said.

"Exactly." Eloise agreed. "I know he can't really do anything from the grave, but his actions once again made a mess for Cameron to clean up."

"She comes from tough stock," Aunt Ginny said. "She'll come through this stronger on the other side."

"A baby is never a mess." Seth fisted his hands.

"Excuse me, Seth?" Seth didn't miss the wink Aunt Ginny sent Eloise.

"I think you know what I said. A baby is never a mess. The situation might be difficult, but you're right. Cameron will pull through. She'll make a wonderful mother."

"I couldn't agree more." His aunt patted his hand, forcing him to unclench his fingers.

"She should have been home by now." *Home.* She

belonged here—with him. "What if she got in an accident? She was so upset when I walked out on her."

"She rode with you, Seth. She wouldn't be driving home alone."

"What if she borrowed someone else's vehicle?"

"Call Caleb and ask him," Aunt Ginny soothed. "He'll know where she is."

Seth thanked the women for their time and input and hurried off to find a quiet place to call Caleb.

"She's fine, Seth. Josie took her back to my place. I don't know if they'll return to the inn or if they'll stay over at the clinic. Cameron was pretty beat up emotionally after you walked out on her."

"I know, Caleb. That's why I'm trying to find her."

"My advice is, let her have some space. Josie's with her, and she'll be fine. Go on out to your cottage, and let them come home in peace. I'll give Josie a heads-up that the coast is clear."

Seth winced. He was the one they wanted to steer clear of. "Are you sure? I need to talk to her."

"She's been through enough tonight. You need time to figure out your end of things. Cameron doesn't need to be let down again. Take some time to think things through before you talk to her. Pray about the situation. Make sure you're willing to be there for the long haul. If you're going to be there for her, you need to be sure you're ready."

Was he ready? He'd taken off like a madman when he found out she was pregnant. He'd jumped to the wrong conclusions. She might not even want to talk to him again. "Great advice, buddy, in all areas. I'll head to the cottage now. Call the ladies, and tell them they can come home. I'll steer clear and will leave Cameron alone." He shut his cell phone and passed through the kitchen.

"'Night, Seth. I'll be prayin' for you and the situation," Eloise called after him. She turned to Aunt Ginny as he walked through the door. Their voices carried after him. "I just figured out what I'll be makin' for my quilt. I'm gonna make a baby quilt out of Cameron's grandfather's shirts."

"What a wonderful idea, El! I'll follow suit and I'll do the same, only I'll make a quilt for Cameron. Mama and baby can both wrap up in a piece of their grandfather's love."

They were already moving on. How did his aunt do that? He was still reeling. The news was new to Aunt Ginny, too, yet she'd already embraced it and was looking ahead to the next step.

Seth understood Cam's reluctance to talk about her marriage. He didn't like to talk about Sylvia either. He unlocked his front door and turned on the light. He sank onto the couch and rested his aching head against the wall. He understood, but still, she could have told him the basics. He'd sat at the dinner table at the Thai restaurant and shared a bit of his engagement to Sylvia. That would have been the perfect opportunity for Cam to share about Jim. Instead, she held it all inside.

He'd gone out on a limb to even date again. Cameron had seemed worth it. But now he had to wonder if dating was worth the heartache. Once again he'd had the rug pulled out from under him. Maybe it would be best to go back to things as they were. He could focus on his work and the renovations, Cameron could focus on delivering babies and raising her own. She hadn't trusted him enough to share the basics of her life with him. Based on that, he didn't think it was a good idea to keep seeing her.

You promised Caleb you'd pray.

He brushed the thought away and pulled a pillow against his chest.

Prayer changes things.

"It isn't like I don't know that," he muttered.

He tossed the pillow aside. "Lord, as usual, I've made a mess of things. Seems every time I get close to a woman, I screw things up. I'm ready to throw in the towel, but if You feel differently about that, You're going to have to show me a sign."

Seth knew he needed to stop comparing Cameron to Sylvia. Sylvia had been stringing him along while she was dating other men. He had faith that Cameron would never do such a thing. Still, trust is trust. When it was broken, it was hard to get back.

He didn't know where his prayers would lead him, but for now, Seth would pray for clarity and direction for his and Cameron's friendship. If God wanted him to give her a second chance, He'd have to make it clear.

Chapter 13

The next morning, Seth had just walked back to the kitchen for a cup of coffee when the front door opened. Squeals of girlish laughter carried down the hall, and he grimaced. His inn had become a breeding ground for womanly pursuits.

He wondered what it was this time. Another quilting bee? A Bible study? A meeting for teen moms? He rounded the corner to gales of laughter and a passel of teens in various stages of pregnancy.

"Pregnancy meeting," he mumbled. It seemed like a bad joke coming on the heels of Cameron's revelation. Pregnant bellies everywhere to remind him of his painful relationship with Cam.

Lord, if this is Your idea of clarity and direction, I'm not finding it funny.

He slipped around the corner, hoping to duck into his office before they saw him.

"Sethie!" One of the girls shrieked. The others giggled, and Seth cringed. With this crew, the nickname would stick. Josie's efforts at bonding the girls together had worked. They'd formed a tight alliance with each other, and what one did, the rest did, too. Or so it seemed.

The pocket doors that opened into the parlor from his office were open, leaving him no privacy. He slipped over to close them.

"Seth!" Josie's perky voice stopped him in his tracks. "Can I bother you to help me with these chairs? The top ones are stuck, and I can't pry them loose."

With a resigned sigh, Seth walked into the masses. "Someone stacked them too high. They're only supposed to be six deep."

"That explains it." Josie tried to help hold the lower chairs, but he waved her off. She stepped back to let him work.

After a few tugs and some muttering, he pried the chairs apart. "Where do you want them?"

"Oh, we can take it from here. I don't want to interrupt more than I already have."

"It's fine. I've got it. The girls don't need to be lifting things like heavy chairs in their condition. Just show me where they need to go."

He looked over to see Cameron facing away from him, lifting a chair from a stack across the room and setting it in position. She certainly didn't need to carry heavy chairs. What was the exasperating woman thinking? "Cam, *stop*."

She glanced over at him with daggers shooting from her puffy eyes. Evidently she'd had time to get past the hurt and move on to anger.

"I'm perfectly capable of moving a few chairs, Seth."

Josie motioned for the girls to leave the room. "Let's go see what we can rustle up in the kitchen for a snack, shall we?"

Cameron rolled her eyes. "You don't need to leave on my account, Josie."

"I'm not." She waved the girls down the hall. "Judging by the look on your face, I'm trying to protect their delicate ears from the yelling."

"No one's going to yell," Seth snapped.

"All the same, I think I'll keep them well away from the war zone. Y'all just take your time and call us when the room's ready."

Seth slammed another chair into place.

Cam gently lifted and settled hers, as if his presence wasn't bothering her. As a matter of fact, she acted as if he weren't in the room at all. As if he hadn't spoken.

"Cameron. I asked you to stop lifting the chairs."

"No." Cam brushed a lock of hair from her flushed face. "You *yelled* for me to stop. I don't respond well to orders or yelling."

He sighed. Pushing her buttons wouldn't solve anything. He forced a dose of calm into his voice. "Cam, will you please stop lifting the chairs and let me do this for you?"

"Sure. It's getting crowded in here anyway. I'll go see if I'm needed in the kitchen."

He blocked her exit before she could make her escape.

She refused to meet his eyes. "First you bark out orders. Now you're going to hold me prisoner?"

"I'm sorry if I offended you—last night and today. I never meant to hurt you. I know we need to talk. Can you give me a few minutes?"

She pulled her cell phone from her pocket and

glanced at the screen. "The meeting is supposed to start in five minutes, and the chairs aren't in place. Some of the parents drop the girls off and are here exactly an hour later to pick them up. I need to start on time."

"Then you round up the girls, and I'll finish setting up the chairs. I'll have them ready when you return."

Seth couldn't tell if her refusal was a brush off or a legitimate reason not to talk. He hurried to set the chairs into place and made a hasty exit into his office. He closed the connecting door and leaned against it with relief.

His celebration was short-lived. He could hear the meeting clearly though the wall.

His office wasn't built for quiet—it was a small sitting area he'd confiscated for his desk. They didn't usually hold meetings in the bigger room, except for the occasional quilting group.

And now he was trapped next to a group-therapy meeting. He decided to double-time his efforts with the city so the girls could move back to Lullaby Landing. Aunt Ginny had started the wheels rolling, but Seth intended to help them along.

Giggles and laughter carried through both doors as the girls filtered back into the room. He sat at his desk and tried to focus on his accounting. The numbers swirled in his brain. He couldn't concentrate with Cameron in the next room and things between them in limbo.

He leaned back in his chair. What did he want from the situation? What had he expected to come of a relationship with Cameron? Did he want a happy-ever-after? Was he looking for a friend?

He shook his head. Of course not. He had plenty of friends. He wanted something more. He wanted a relationship and, hopefully, marriage and a family. But a baby? A baby changed everything. A baby meant forever.

Cameron's soft voice carried through the door. "Caleb has asked us to speak to the youth group at church, and I'd like each of you to give your personal perspective on pregnancy. Yes, Mandy?"

"What do you mean by 'personal perspective'?"

"I just want you to share your story in a natural way. For instance, how many of you became pregnant the first time you had sex?"

Seth wondered if he should leave, but if they were going to speak publicly to the youth about the topic, this information wasn't exactly secret. The rustle of hands being raised filtered through the door.

He shook his head. They were so young. They had their whole lives ahead of them. Now they would have to fight for everything they got out of life—though for most of the girls, that was nothing new. Most of them had been scraping along on their own for the better part of their lives. Now they'd be scraping for two. They deserved to catch a break.

"How many of you were pushed into having sex and thought it was the only way to hold on to your guy? How many had boyfriends that used the 'if you love me' line?"

More rustling of hands. Seth's blood began to boil.

"I want you to know you aren't alone in your experiences. Even older women can have unplanned pregnancies from one bad choice. Women like—me."

The girls sat in stunned silence.

"I was married, but barely. We'd been separated for over a year. My husband wanted the divorce, then he wanted to reconcile. I felt it was the right thing to try. I mean, everyone deserves a second chance, right?"

The girls murmured their agreement.

The words hit Seth like a boulder. *Everyone deserves a second chance.* Was it a coincidence that Cameron had used the exact words Seth had prayed the night before? Had she used them for his benefit? He doubted it. She had no idea he could hear them from the other side of the wall or that he'd even stayed in the office. She most likely hadn't given him another thought.

Seth felt like God had spoken directly to him through Cameron's words.

He had hurt her deeply when he refused to listen. He'd based his reaction to Cameron's pregnancy on a bad experience with Sylvia. But Cameron was no Sylvia. Cameron was loyal to a fault, caring, and her apparent downfall was trying too hard with a man she'd made a commitment to.

Sylvia, on the other hand, was conniving, deceitful, and disloyal. When her house of cards fell down around her, she admitted that she'd sneaked around on him throughout their entire relationship.

Cameron hadn't done anything wrong. He needed to give her a second chance. Or rather, he hoped she'd see fit to give him a second chance.

He huffed out a breath and prayed he wasn't too late.

Against his better judgment, he walked to the pocket doors and slid them open.

"I'm sorry for listening in, but the walls are really thin." He addressed his apology to Cameron and Josie then turned his attention to the girls. "You're speaking to the youth group. Matt, Caleb, and I will be there, too. And all the boys from the youth group. Just so you know I'm not hearing anything I won't hear that evening. And what you'll be saying…definitely needs to be heard by the boys."

Cameron stood at the front of the room, staring at him. He couldn't quite read her expression.

He cleared his throat. "If I might say a few words on behalf of the males who aren't here to defend themselves—or more importantly, set things right for you?"

"Go ahead"—Cameron motioned him to the front of the room—"though some of our meetings do cover things that the girls would rather not have random males listening in on."

"Point taken." Seth took Cameron's place at the front. "I would have run the other way if the topic went dicey."

"No surprise there," one of the girls quipped.

"Typical man," said another.

"See, that's just why I'm here." Seth gave the girl a pointed look. "I'm here to speak up for the males who aren't here to make their own statements. There are a lot of typical men out there, but I, for one, don't like the concept. I don't like to be lumped into the mix or dumped into a category."

The girls quieted. He had their full attention.

"You didn't get into this situation on your own. I get that. And while you all can take some of the responsibility, I feel the guys need to take more. Let me get one thing out of the way up front." He breathed a quick prayer for the right words. "The first thing you need to know is that any guy who puts sexual pressure on you—any guy who puts you into an uncool situation of any kind—isn't worth dating. It doesn't matter how popular he is. It doesn't matter how cute he is. If a guy pressures you in any way—if he pulls the lame 'if you love me you'll do this'—run. Get away from him right then. If he says other girls are waiting on the sidelines and if you don't put out, they will—tell him to get lost. Make your stand and don't back down."

He paused to look into each girl's eyes. "Even better, don't pick a guy like that in the first place. I'm sure Josie and Brit and Cameron can help you figure out ways to troubleshoot who to date and who not to. But a good rule of thumb to start with is, if other people are urging you to rethink your choices, you'd be smart to listen to them. Keep a support group around you who can keep you in line."

He had their rapt attention. "If you wait, the right guy who is mature and who truly loves you will come along. If you're open to God's blessing, the timing will work out as God desires. And the right guy will want to marry you and commit to you for life."

A mixture of hope and doubt played out on their faces. Mandy spoke up. "We've already messed things up when it comes to that. What guy wants to be saddled with someone else's child? Even the fathers of most of these babies don't want them."

Seth's heart ached for the girls. "Then it'll be their loss and someone else's gain."

"You really believe that?"

"I know it from experience." He looked at Cameron as he said the words. "The right guy will cling to the idea of a baby like he plans to cling to the idea of loving the baby's mama forever. He'll know you're a package deal, and if he's a smart man, he'll be anxious to embrace it."

Cameron's eyes looked watery, and she jumped to her feet. "Okay, I think Seth has made some great points. Seth"—she choked up—"we appreciate your coming here and sharing the insights from a male point of view. We don't get enough of that, and I think it's something we need to work in on a regular basis."

Seth knew when he was being dismissed. He headed for the front hall, intent on making a clean getaway.

"Not so fast, wise guy." Josie followed him out the front door and onto the porch. "Was that what I think it was?"

"What do you think it was?"

"I'm thinking if I'm not sure, Cameron won't be sure either. You had some good things to say in there, but I also think you and Cam need to have a nice heart-to-heart."

"I agree. I've asked, she's avoided."

"I think if you ask again, she'll agree."

He hoped Josie was right. "I'll ask as soon as the meeting is over. As a matter of fact, you can do me a favor and ask her for me."

"No way." Josie took a step back, her hands in the air. "I'm not getting in the middle of this any more than I already am."

"All I ask is that you snag her before she sneaks away."

"She lives here, Seth. Where's she gonna go?"

"She got away last night."

"*You* got away last night. She was devastated. She'd been publicly humiliated in front of her friends, and the person she cares about the most ran out on her."

Her words punched him in the gut. "I'm not proud of my actions."

"I know." Josie laid a hand on his arm. "I think everyone understands, especially now that a few more pieces of the puzzle have come together through Caleb and Ginny and Eloise."

"Aunt Ginny talked to Cameron?"

"She actually said Cameron needed to hear you out. But we got enough information to formulate a picture of what you went through with Sylvia."

Seth smirked. "The ladies have been busy. They started their evening explaining a few things to me."

"So you agree that it's time you and Cam lost the go-betweens and sat down to speak for yourselves?"

"I agree. I'll be waiting down by the lake. Tell her to meet me on my boat. Send her my way if she'll come. Or if she wants, we can go somewhere else, somewhere away from the house."

"I'll let her know. She'll be there, or I'll call you after the meeting."

Seth headed for the water. The dock was his refuge. His boat rested in its stall along with the rentals for the guests of the inn. Seth jumped aboard, mindless of the cool air blowing across the water. He had an idea. He ducked below the deck and started a pot of coffee. The boat would give them a private place to talk. He might even take her out on the water.

One way or another, Cameron was going to listen to what he had to say.

The dock rocked under Cameron's feet. She saw no signs of Seth and wondered if Josie had misunderstood. But her friend wasn't prone to missing important details.

Dusk was falling, the sky awash with pastel colors. Water lapped against the sides of the boats, shifting them in the water. The evening was warm for October, but once complete darkness arrived, the air would quickly cool.

Cameron hugged her jacket around her. "Seth?"

"Down here." She couldn't ignore the excitement in his voice. "Hang on. I'll help you onto the boat."

Stairs creaked to her right. Seth appeared on deck.

He reached for her hand, and her skin tingled. She stepped onto the deck and looked around. "I guess I never really thought about these boats belonging to the inn."

"They don't. Well, this one doesn't. This one's mine. The jet skis, kayaks, and the fishing boats belong to the inn."

"Which belongs to you, so inadvertently they're all yours."

He grinned. "Something like that."

She quieted, not sure what to say.

"Come below deck. I wanted to make sure we talked in private. I don't want anyone to overhear."

"Like today in the meeting?"

He grinned sheepishly. "I said I would have left if things got dicey. But no, I was referring to the public arena of your outing at the mini golf place." He took both her hands in his. "I'm sorry for abandoning you. I'm sorry for my behavior. I'm sorry for the public announcement."

"You weren't responsible for that part."

"No, but it all ties in together. I'm still sorry it happened."

"Me, too." She glanced around and headed for the stairs. Christian praise music played quietly through hidden speakers. A battery-powered candle lit the table, giving the cabin a warm glow. "Oh—it's much nicer down here."

"I tried." Seth motioned her to the curved booth that surrounded the table. "Have a seat."

Cameron slid into place. Seth handed her a bottled

water. "If you're hungry, I have cheese and crackers and some fruit."

"Maybe in a bit."

"Then I'll get on with it. Where was I? Oh yeah, the apologies."

She quieted him with a hand. "You've said your apologies. I accept. Now I need to say mine."

"You don't have anything to apologize for."

"Yes, I do. I shouldn't have kept any of my past from you. You shared with me about your broken engagement." She looked at her hands. "I should have opened up about my failed marriage."

"Eloise explained things last night. I'm sorry for jumping to conclusions and thinking the worst about you."

"You had a right to, after what Sylvia did."

"No. You aren't Sylvia. You aren't anything like her."

"I can see how you didn't know that though. Yes, I wanted a fresh start, but when our relationship started to grow, I should have told you the full story. I had nothing to gain from keeping it from you."

"You gained peace."

"Temporary peace. I panicked when you showed up at the estate, knowing you'd find out my story. But then it never came up, and I figured why ruin a good thing that early in the game?"

"You thought I'd think less of you if I knew you'd been married?"

"Some men prefer not to marry a divorcée or a widow."

"We're talking marriage now?" He teased.

She blushed. "I'm talking in the abstract. Most people date with the intent to find someone to marry."

"Point taken. I'm sorry if I embarrassed you." He shifted. "I'm not handling this very well, am I?"

She ignored his question. "All that said, where does that leave us? My belly is growing bigger, seemingly overnight. Most men wouldn't want to date a pregnant woman."

"I'm not most men."

"I'm okay with us remaining friends."

"I'm not."

Cameron's stomach took a tumble. She studied his face. His gaze didn't waver from hers. "You still want to date me?"

He smiled, and his dimple appeared. "Why do you find that surprising?"

"I'm going to have a baby."

"Lots of women have babies."

"Yes, lots of women have babies—with their husbands."

"Look, Cam." Seth took both her hands in his. The candlelight glowed off the highlights in his hair. His aquamarine eyes radiated warmth as he stared into hers. "We've both made mistakes based on hurts in the past. We're both ready to move on. There's a baby coming, who adds dimension to the big picture. We aren't unprepared teens, wondering what to do next. We're both established. We love our town. We love our lives. And I think I can safely say we've grown to love each other."

He waited for her answer.

Tears trickled down her cheeks. Not trusting her voice, she could only nod.

"I don't want this baby to be born without a father. I don't want you to give birth without a husband. I don't want you to go through this alone."

She choked on a sob. "Are you asking me to marry you?"

He grinned, his eyes sparkling. "In a confusing and roundabout way, yes. I know we need more time to get to know each other. But I also know I've spent enough time over the past few months to know you're the one for me."

"You didn't seem to know it last night."

"I knew it long before last night. Last night threw me for a loop. It made me dig deep to evaluate where we stood in a way I wouldn't have had to if there hadn't been a baby involved. Fact is, there is a baby involved, and he isn't going to wait for us to get our acts together before he makes an appearance."

"Before *she* makes her appearance." She removed her hands from his to wipe her eyes. "And I don't want to rush into anything."

"I don't either." He took her hands again. He didn't seem to mind the dampness. "But I think we're both okay with going in the same direction. We can stumble along the path together."

"I agree."

He looked around the small cabin. "I don't have anything fancy to celebrate with, but I do have sparkling cider."

"Sounds good to me."

He pulled out the cider and a couple of crystal goblets. They toasted to new beginnings.

Before she had time to take a sip, he pulled her to her feet, wrapped his arms around her, and gave her a kiss worth waiting for.

Epilogue

Caleb walked to the front of the church and motioned for everyone to stand. Seth took Cameron's arm and helped her to her feet. Cameron allowed her new husband to assist her as she nestled their newborn daughter, Ginelle, tightly against her chest.

She stepped into the aisle. Aunt Ginny and Eloise smiled with pride as Seth and Cameron passed by with their namesake. Alfie stepped back to let the ladies pass. They fell into place behind Seth and Cameron.

Across the way, Brian helped Sailor to her feet. Their baby boy, Max—already nearing five months old—cooed and gurgled as he tried to catch his father's attention. Brian smiled indulgently and chucked the baby on the chin. Max lunged into his father's arms. Brian held him close.

Mandy stood next, and Josie handed her a pink wrapped bundle. The group headed for the front of the church as a family unit. Brian and Sailor hadn't yet tied the knot, but the wedding date had been set.

Allie and her family met them at the front. Brit's engagement ring sparkled as she waved at Cameron. Allie's baby girl grabbed for the microphone, and everyone laughed.

Caleb let her wrap her fingers around his larger finger as he turned to face the audience. "I'd like to welcome you all to the first baby dedication sponsored by Lullaby Landing."

Everyone in the audience clapped.

"As you all know, we've had a few glitches over the past year that caused the center to open later than expected."

The crowd murmured.

"But we're open again and filling up fast. Word of mouth has clients coming from nearby towns to take advantage of our facilities. The ministry is up and running. Now, if I can get my wife over here to join me"— he motioned Josie to his side—"I'd like to say a prayer over the families who braved the first year at the clinic."

"Amen to that!" The pastor called from the front row. He stood to join Caleb, and Caleb handed him the microphone. "Don't you have some news of your own to share before we pray?" Pastor Gary asked.

"I do." Caleb looked lovingly at Josie. "Josie and I will have a special delivery of our own this coming year. We're having a baby in the fall."

The congregation clapped and cheered.

Cameron looked over at Seth, and he smiled. He

wrapped an arm around her and pulled her tight against his side.

Cameron couldn't think of any place she'd rather be.

* * * * *

REQUEST YOUR FREE BOOKS!

2 FREE CHRISTIAN NOVELS
PLUS 2
FREE
MYSTERY GIFTS

HEARTSONG
PRESENTS

YES! Please send me 2 Free Heartsong Presents novels and my 2 FREE mystery gifts (gifts are worth about $10). After receiving them, if I don't wish to receive any more books I can return the shipping statement marked "cancel." If I don't cancel, I will receive 4 brand-new novels every month and be billed just $4.24 per book. That's a savings of 20% off the cover price. It's quite a bargain! Shipping and handling is just 50¢ per book in the U.S.* I understand that accepting the 2 free books and gifts places me under no obligation to buy anything. I can always return a shipment and cancel at any time. Even if I never buy another book, the two free books and gifts are mine to keep forever.

159 HDN FT97

Name	(PLEASE PRINT)

Address	Apt. #

City	State	Zip

Signature (if under 18, a parent or guardian must sign)

Mail to the **Reader Service:**
IN U.S.A.: P.O. Box 1867, Buffalo, NY 14240-1867

Not valid for current subscribers to Heartsong Presents books.

* Terms and prices subject to change without notice. Prices do not include applicable taxes. Sales tax applicable in N.Y. This offer is limited to one order per household. All orders subject to credit approval. Credit or debit balances in a customer's account(s) may be offset by any other outstanding balance owed by or to the customer. Please allow 4 to 6 weeks for delivery. Offer available while quantities last. Offer valid only in the U.S.

Your Privacy—The Reader Service is committed to protecting your privacy. Our Privacy Policy is available online at www.ReaderService.com or upon request from the Reader Service.

We make a portion of our mailing list available to reputable third parties that offer products we believe may interest you. If you prefer that we not exchange your name with third parties, or if you wish to clarify or modify your communication preferences, please visit us at www.ReaderService.com/consumerschoice or write to us at Reader Service Preference Service, P.O. Box 9062, Buffalo, NY 14269. Include your complete name and address.

REQUEST YOUR FREE BOOKS!

2 FREE INSPIRATIONAL NOVELS
PLUS 2
FREE
MYSTERY GIFTS

YES! Please send me 2 FREE Love Inspired® novels and my 2 FREE mystery gifts (gifts are worth about $10). After receiving them, if I don't wish to receive any more books, I can return the shipping statement marked "cancel." If I don't cancel, I will receive 6 brand-new novels every month and be billed just $4.49 per book in the U.S. or $4.99 per book in Canada. That's a savings of at least 22% off the cover price. It's quite a bargain! Shipping and handling is just 50¢ per book in the U.S. and 75¢ per book in Canada.* I understand that accepting the 2 free books and gifts places me under no obligation to buy anything. I can always return a shipment and cancel at any time. Even if I never buy another book, the two free books and gifts are mine to keep forever.

105/305 IDN FVW5

Name _____ (PLEASE PRINT) _____

Address _____ Apt. # _____

City _____ State/Prov. _____ Zip/Postal Code _____

Signature (if under 18, a parent or guardian must sign) _____

Mail to the **Reader Service:**
IN U.S.A.: P.O. Box 1867, Buffalo, NY 14240-1867
IN CANADA: P.O. Box 609, Fort Erie, Ontario L2A 5X3

**Are you a subscriber to Love Inspired books
and want to receive the larger-print edition?
Call 1-800-873-8635 or visit www.ReaderService.com.**

* Terms and prices subject to change without notice. Prices do not include applicable taxes. Sales tax applicable in N.Y. Canadian residents will be charged applicable taxes. Offer not valid in Quebec. This offer is limited to one order per household. Not valid for current subscribers to Love Inspired books. All orders subject to credit approval. Credit or debit balances in a customer's account(s) may be offset by any other outstanding balance owed by or to the customer. Please allow 4 to 6 weeks for delivery. Offer available while quantities last.

Your Privacy—The Reader Service is committed to protecting your privacy. Our Privacy Policy is available online at www.ReaderService.com or upon request from the Reader Service.

We make a portion of our mailing list available to reputable third parties that offer products we believe may interest you. If you prefer that we not exchange your name with third parties, or if you wish to clarify or modify your communication preferences, please visit us at www.ReaderService.com/consumerchoice or write to us at Reader Service Preference Service, P.O. Box 9062, Buffalo, NY 14269. Include your complete name and address.